HEALING OUR SOULS

Matilda Talbot

Contents

Prologue

"I will show what I will do to you if you disobey me as you are not liking my good side", he shouted at me and I was shivering by seeing his dangerous glaring eyes which held no remorse. He was cold, arrogant and has no emotions.

He dragged me by holding my wrist tightly which is already bruised, with stumbling feet I followed him as he is walking fast. I cant catch up with his speed as I fall down he left my hand and glared at me. I cower back in fear as what he will do to me. I was shivering and crying very badly by seeing him.

"I will make your life hell because of what you did to me. I will never forget and forgive for your mistakes, Get that in your head. You will pay for your sins and God will never forgive you. You are a murderer", He spills venom through his mouth and dragged me on the floor from living hall to the kitchen. I am feeling pain in every part of my body but I cant open my mouth as fear crept inside me and my body became numb.

He lifted me up by my shoulders but my body is weak as I cannot stand by myself and leaned onto him.I want to say I cannot bear his tortures anymore. But before that he held my right hand and placed it in the hot water as it was on the stove. I screamed in horror, pain and have no words left my mouth.

"Ah...ahh... ahh mumma", I screamed loudly as it was unbearable and I pushed the pan from the stove and it fell down opposite side with the boiling water.

"Please lea..ve me, I am rea....lly so sorry dont do thii...is, I will obey your orders Sir", I stuttered as he held my left hand more tightly. As I was feeling dizzy I leaned onto him by holding his shoulder with my right hand. I thought this will be my last day on mother earth. Unstoppable tears flowed through my eyes.

"Please help me, let me die in peace", As I uttered those words by staring at him directly, darkness consumed me.

"It hurts, Isn't it? But what is my mistake in this that you gave me unbearable pain throughout my life which i can never forget. You will pay for every pain I went through", He whispered maliciously in my ear by holding me by my waist as I was unconscious. I did not heard any word said by him.

Life After Marriage

Nikshitra's Pov:

I am sitting on the bed for past half an hour as it was my first night after marriage. I am hell nervous as I am fidgeting with my fingers. I dont know what he gonna do. I am so scared as I dont know if he want to take next step of our marriage. I think I am not ready for this. I think I will ask him to give me some time. Several thoughts are running in my mind. I want to ask him so many questions but I dont know how I will ask him as I met him only once before marriage.

I dont know why he asked me to marry him as he came to my house that day. He is very handsome and a billionaire. I dont know what he does as my father trusts him very much so I said yes for this marriage. His black eyes are so captivating that I can see every minute. His million dollar smile can capture many girls. I know I am dreaming about him everyday as I am falling for him.

I am a average mediocre girl with average looks and slim body. I have completed my graduation this year so my dad want me to settle down. As in settle down means to get married, So here I am.

"Oh God.."I was in my thoughts when the door opened and entered my handsome husband. There my husband standing in white kurta looking more handsome than he is. I was staring at him continuously as he marched towards me. He glared at me as I dont know why he is glaring at me. As he was smiling a while ago with my father.

He held my left hand which is on my lap and pulled me from the bed. I was shocked by his action as I fell down on the floor. He did not gave me time as my shock filled and widened eyes are staring and asking questions of what did I do wrong?

"What are you doing and how dare you to treat me like this?" I asked as tears gathered in my eyes. Unable to get up as my leg twisted in this process. With the help of bed I slowly got up from the floor and glared at him.

"How dare you to sit on my bed and who gave permission to you. Who do you think you are? You are already acting like a queen. I know you are a whore who sleeps with many men for money. Your innocent looks cant fool me. You Gold digger slut", he insulted me instead of answering my previous questions. I was dumbfounded by his accusations. How can he accuse me like that? What does he know about me. The tears which were gathered in my eyes started flowing listening to his accusations.

"You know what I will tell you what is your place", he smirked at me and I was shocked by his behaviour. I cant utter any word as I was numb hearing his accusations. I felt so much pain as nobody insulted me in this way. Never in my life I felt this much pain. As I am dad's only daughter he pampered me very much and looked after my every need.

"You will sleep on the floor but not in this room" I got scared as what he will do to me. He sweetly smiled at me and got infront of me. There was no gap inbetween us as I widened my eyes,he put his hand on one side of my waist and lifted me by my waist on his shoulders like a potato sack up in no time.

"Please put me down. Please leave me. Let me go" I screamed and started to beat him on his back as I was upside down and he gave no reaction to it. He did not budge a bit and gave no heed to it. I was hitting him but he seemed to not care a little bit as he was huge built. So I started pinching him to get a reaction from him.

"If you do not stop I will slap you. Do you get that?" He screamed at me and I was shocked at his anger. He will slap me if I do not listen to him, can he do that? I was terrified and kept my mouth shut.

He walked fast and put me down infront of a room. The door is locked and he unlocked the door and pushed me into that room with his hands as i was glaring him. He locked the door within a second as I stumbled on my feet and got hit by a wooden box which is on the way. The room was dark as I cannot see anything.

I ran fast to the door before closing but to my bad luck I was collided with the door.

"Open the door please.. It is very dark. I am sorry. I dont know what mistake I did but I am sorry. Please get me out from this room. Please open the door. I request you." I was crying very badly as I dont know why he is doing like this to me. I will ask him as he cannot do this to me. Why did he say those awful words to me. What was my mistake?

I slid down to the floor by keeping my both hands on the door. I was silently crying till now hugging my knees with both hands. I was disappointed by myself as I did not fight back with him. I speak less as I am introvert. I dont know how to interact with people. But I know I cant live my life like this. I have to do something. My dad was very happy seeing my marriage because of my dad I agreed to this marriage as I cant burden him anymore.

I removed my jewellery and kept it on top of the wooden box. I slept on the floor weeping silently curling into a ball. Due to tiredness sleep consumed me.

Slap

Nikshitra's Pov :

Bright sunlight rays fall into the room through window and I woke up squinting my eyes to recognise as where I am. I remembered last night events and my eyes started to water. So I gathered myself and thought to myself that I should not cry and I wiped my eyes to not cry anymore. As my eyes are already swollen due to lots of crying since yesterday as it is paining.

Slowly I got up from the floor and made my mind to confront him. How can he do this to me as I am his wife. He will answer every question to me as I will not leave him without answering. I am determined to solve this problem by anyways.

"Oh god please help me as I am going to devil's den. Please make it possible to confront him. I am so scared of what he will do to me if he is angry. So please god dont make him angry" I sent a prayer to god and went towards the door. I opened the door as it was unlocked. I dont know when he unlocked the door and searched for his room not making any sound.

One door was slightly opened which I recognised as his room from yesterday.

I slowly opened the door and entered into his room. Only footsteps sound can be heard as it was very silent in the room. No one was there in the room. The place was same from yesterday nothing has changed. The decorations still not removed which was made for our first night. I dont know where is he and then I heard the sound of door click the he came in front of me only in towel which is hanging below his waist. I can see his mouth watering six abs. He is well built and with my widened eyes I was staring his body continuosly without any shame.

"You... how dare you come into my room. What are you seeing. I know I am handsome but you dont have any right to see my body. I know you are shameless as you have slept with so many men. You whore" he walked to me within two long strides in a second and hold my bare waist tightly with his two hands leaving no gap between us. As water drop fall from his hair on my cheek I came out of dream-land. His eyes colour changed and he was staring at me longingly. I was afraid so I pushed him with my hands to let me go but he did not budge a bit. I stared down to avoid him. As I thought of his words from before a tear fell from my left eye. As I know he thinks of me shameless as I was staring at his body. I dont know what happened to me a while ago. I think it is because I have not seen any male in towel.

"Please let me go I am sorry. I dont know you were showering Ayush. I will never do that again. Leave me..." I kept my both hands on his chest to push him but he did otherwise. He slowly leaned onto my face closing his eyes. He was rubbing my bare waist with his both hands and slowly inhaled my cheek with his nose. His nose was touching my right cheek and I closed my eyes savouring the moment. His touches makes me senseless as wherever he touched I felt tingling sensation. My heart beat raced and I was heavily breathing as I thought he will kiss me but nothing like that happened as he was only inhaling me.

After few minutes I felt a push and I stumbled but balanced myself and opened my eyes to see him turned backwards to me with his fists clenched. I dont know what happened to him.

Then after few seconds he turned towards me glaring and spoke the words which I can never forget in my life.

"Why did you not got up early in the morning who will do the works. You think any maids are there for you in the house. If you think like that then you are wrong. I will say what is your position in this house. You are the maid of this house. And you will be my slave till you die. Do you get that" He shouted at me and I shivered at his loud voice. But who does he think is he. I am not his maid. He thinks whatever he says I will silently listen to him. No, I will fight back and I will not do any work for him as I thought in my mind and I started to speak.

"I will not do any work in your house as I am your wife. Who do you think you are? why are you treating me like this? I am tolerating your nonsense from yesterday what is my mistake? Why are you yelling that I am a whore. Have you seen me with any men? Tell me?" I shouted at the end instead of answering me he slapped me hard. Due to the hit I fall down on the floor keeping my right hand on my right cheek. My lips are bleeding at one side of my mouth. He is behaving like a beast. A while ago he behaved differently and now he slapped me.

My widened eyes and tears flowing from my both eyes did nothing to him.

"Listen carefully you piece of shit, You will only call me SIR. You dont have any right to call me by my name. You are low class girl who cant even be compare to my standards. As you are here I can see what a gold digger you are. You have to follow my rules to live here if not I will remove your father's job. As I know the owner of your father's company, he will fire him within a minute. It is your decision." I was shocked hearing his statement. I am afraid for my father as he can do anything as he said. I cant speak any word as my situation is worse.

"You will get up early at 5 am and do all the house chore duties cleaning, washing, cooking, mopping, laundry and everything. You cannot go outside without my permission. You will not get any money from me. Only for groceries I will give you the money and nothing more than that. You will go with the driver and bodyguard and will return home directly. Is that clear? If not I know many ways to punish you. It will be more dangerous for you. Say yes or I will start with your punishment" he shouted and smirked at the end. He was devil in disguise. He is two faced monster. His handprints will be clear on my cheek as I can feel the pain.

I got up from the floor and walked to the room without turning towards him. As I can feel he is coming towards me. Fastly I was locking the door but before that he entered into my room and marched towards me. Going backwards I hit the wall without noticing, he hit his both hands on the wall either side of my face. I got frightened and I was not seeing at him. My eyes are downwards as I was shivering badly due to the fear of him. Suddenly he grabbed my hair tightly, I winced and hold his hand with my both hands to let go of me.

"Never ever go without answering me. You will face the worst consequences. Do you understand?" He whispered menacingly with each and every word clear. I nodded slowly but still he did not leave my hair as it is becoming difficult to bear the pain.

"Words" He growled, gripped my hair more tightly and my loud sobs and crying can be heard throughout the room. But it did not do anything to him.

"Yes" I slowly said to him.

"SIR, who will say that" he spoke to me harshly.

"Yes Sir, I will do all works" I spoke timidly and then he left my hair afterwards. My scalp is paining very much and I slide down on the wall crying profusely. He left from there loudly banging the door shut.

" Why my life bacame like this" I thought and started to get ready to do the duties.

His Plan

Ayush's Pov:

Three months ago

"Did you get any information about her? I want to hear positive news from you otherwise you can leave from here. There is no use to stand and repeat same thing since nine months" I asked the PI (Private Investigator) angrily who is standing frightened in front of me in my office.

"Yes Sir and sorry for the delay as I know only little from the past. It has taken time to search for her as I found it difficult to get through her college. I have every detail of that girl Sir. Here is the file. Her past and present and her family every detail is present in this file Sir." He said proudly as he failed every single time in nine months and he got the right information this time. He passed the file to me.

"Good and this better be right otherwise you know what I will do you" I smirked and opened the cheque book and gave the cheque to him. I know with the amount written there he will be more than satisfied. He smiled brightly after seeing the amount and left from my cabin hurriedly after saying thank you.

"Now let the game begin" I thought to myself and opened the file in which an average looking girl photo appeared dressed in light purple chudidhar smiling brightly with big black eyes shining brightly. I turned the page and read about her. Her name is Nikshitra. What a beautiful name I thought. In one month her graduation will be completed. Her family consists of only her father. Her mother died while giving birth to her. Middle class family where her father works in a private company with less salary. No permanent residence as they are living on rent near local society. No boyfriends, No affairs are written there but I know what a characterless girl she is.

I closed the file after reading every single detail about her. As I am a billionaire I can get everything in the snap of my fingers. I have many businesses all over the world. My company is the biggest one in this city.

"Now the plan begins. Welcome to the hell Nikshitra as you don't know what is waiting for you. I will make you mine and make you pay for every sin you did in your life" I smirked and spoke to myself staring at the view in front of me through the glass mirror.

Present:

As I thought her father trusted me and gave her daughter to me. He did not even once reject my proposal as I am a billionaire. I directly went to her father and said I loved her daughter for a very long time. I asked for her hand in marriage. I did not speak to her at that time when I met her father. After a week of my proposal her father told me to meet nikshitra as it will be her decision.

She was very happy by seeing me as she was smiling brightly now and then. I know what a great actress she is. She is acting very innocent. But I am not a fool to fell into her trap. She was nervous at that time as I can say through her fidgeting with the fingers. She only asked to take care of her father's expenses as there is no one other than her. I accepted her condition easily as I wanted my plan to succeed. I was internally smirking at that time. She also got into my sugar coated words and trusted me very easily as I said I will bear all the expenses of her father from now on. As I told her it will be a registered marriage she nodded happily as they have no relatives other than her and her father. I told her only my friend will be present there as a witness to sign other than that no one was there for me. She looked sad for a moment while I spoke about my family.

As there is no engagement I prepared the marriage date after a month. As no doubt arose I bought her wedding saree and jewellery. I sent it through my driver before a week of my marriage.

One month went by really fast as my marriage day arrived. I dressed in a black suit and white shirt underneath with black tie and black trouser. I was ready and directly went to the registration office by 11am. They also came after 5 minutes. She was looking beautiful in that red saree but I know outer appearances can fool anyone but not me as I know what a girl she is.

Within an hour marriage rituals are completed. Witness signatures are done by my friend Sameer and her dad.

"I will take care of her Uncle. You dont need to worry about her. I will give her everything she needs. I love her very much Uncle. Thank you for trusting me Uncle. Then we will meet soon Uncle" I directly stared at her dad and convinced her father that I will take care of her very well. She cried a lot while leaving her dad hugging him tightly. She was not ready to leave her dad so I patiently waited and said to her dad that I will take care of her from now on.

"Now you have to leave your dad as I will take care of everything from now onwards. If any problem arises I will be there with you. You will be happy with me. I know it will take some time to understand each other but I know we will make through it. Now lets say bye to your dad" I avoided her eyes purposely while talking to her. Then I held her left hand with my right hand and felt a tingling sensation in my body but I ignored it and dragged her from there till my car. I opened the passenger door for her and she silently sat in the car weeping.

I was silent throughout the drive as I know she will not stop crying if I said anything to her. I think she is expecting me to console her. But I dont give a damn about her. After reaching my mansion I turned towards her as I can see she is not moving but only staring my mansion with wide eyes. I internally laughed as she will remember this house for lifetime. Without bothering her, I patiently waited as when she will get down. Is she thinking I will open the car door for her. In her dreams.

"Get down" I said and opened my side of the door and shut it loudly. Without even glancing at her I went directly to my office.

With clenching jaw I stride fast towards my mansion. I dont want to see her face but I have to tolerate. I was feeling very angry towards her as I cant do anymore acting. By seeing her my temper is rising. But I know what I have to do.

I was working in my office till midnight. When I went to my room I got very angry as she is sitting on my bed thinking deeply. She did noticed me after hearing the door sound. I have to be harsh from the beginning only otherwise she thinks she can rule me. No, it will never happen in this lifetime. So I showed her place where she belongs in my life.

Regret

Ayush Pov:

I told the maids to decorate my bedroom for the first night as I don't know if her father or Sameer comes to my house. It will be difficult to explain the situation so I prepared beforehand.

She was not looking towards me as I was in front of her. She started seeing her lap with her eyes down. I got angry as I remembered what she did and I pulled her from the bed and she fell down.

She surprised me when I thought she will not fight back but she fought back with me. As I can see she is holding her tears back due to the pain in the leg but I have to see her tears to feel peace. As my mind is saying she deserves the pain but my heart says otherwise. But I listened to my mind as I know whatever I am doing is right.

I insulted her with bad names so she can feel the pain of what I went through. I carried her to the last room which is dark and no one uses it as it was empty. She started screaming, beating me with her small hands which never affected me and now she started pinching me, I got startled by her action and I threatened to slap her then she kept quiet. She banged the door so many times after I pushed her into the room. I left from there not bothering about her banging. I can hear her sobbing and screaming.

I left from there, slept peacefully on my bed without removing the decorations as I was very tired.

I woke up as the alarm rang and washed my face to get away from the sleep. I unlocked her room door before going to my personal gym early in the morning. After 1 hour of gym I went directly to freshen up as my body is sweaty. When I returned from showering she was staring with her wide eyes.

I scolded her and she avoided my eyes. I was looking at her face as she was looking innocent with swollen red eyes. The cute pout of her made me feel different emotions. As I came in front of her, I touched her waist with my cold hand. She was very warm and I didn't want to leave her. I rubbed her bare waist and made circles around her soft skin.

"Look at me" I said as I wanted to kiss her as my eyes clouded with lust. She is looking so beautiful in that saree without any traces of makeup and no jewellery. Only the nuptial chain is on her neck which made me proud by seeing it. Her hands on my chest made me feel warm on my cold body. Her touch is making me feel tingles. Seeing her round cheeks I inched my face closer to her right cheek closing my eyes, inhaling her scent. My nose touched her cheek. Then and there I wanted to kiss her cheek but I managed to control my emotions and realised what I was doing. I pushed her and turned my back towards her.

How can I do this? What was I thinking? How can I fall for her looks? No, I have to control my emotions. This is not right. I have to be harsh with her then I cannot feel these things.

In anger I said many things. When she asked the question as I have seen any male with her, I do not want to remember the past things anytime. My painful moments came in front of my eyes. I thought about how my life changed because of her sin. Then in anger my right hand hit her hard on her cheek without realising. I regretted that moment when I slapped her.

But I know she deserves it. I changed my expression from hurt to glare when she turned to me. A small part of me regrets slapping her as I can see my handprints are visible on her smooth skin.

I maintained my posture so as to not reveal I was hurt seeing her in pain. I became heartless and set the rules for her to follow. I know she is afraid of me as I can feel her fear towards me. She is shivering but I did not pay attention to it as I cannot fall into her trap. She will get used to it as she will be here for a lifetime.

Atlast she listened to me when I threatened her with her fathers job. I know she cannot go anywhere till I want. My plan succeeded.

"Clean my room and remove all the decorations and prepare my breakfast before 8 as I dont want to be late for my office." I ordered her and left without glancing at her.

Nikshitra's Pov:

As I entered the bathroom I realized I didn't have my clothes with me. With that I frowned at how to ask that devil to get my clothes.

Will he bring my clothes and now what should I wear. There is not much time to prepare his breakfast.

I entered his room after gaining little confidence as the door was open. I couldn't speak standing in front of him as he was looking like a greek god with a blue fitted tailored suit and his features sharpened with his little beard appearing on his jaw. His cold expression turned me into a jelly.

"I..I..I wa..nt I..", I stuttered nervously as the fear of him did not go away.

"Speak fast. I don't have time for all your nonsense. If you can't speak, go away from here", I got scared listening to his loud voice. But I have to get my clothes. With small courage I again tried to speak.

"I don't have my clothes with me. I don't have anything to wear other than this wedding dress. I ha..ve packed it. It is there in my dad's house. Can you help me bring the clothes?"I asked timidly and explained my situation as he was looking without blinking once. I think he came out of his trance and went to his closet. Then he came out after a few minutes with his black track and white shirt.

"Now wear this. I will tell my driver to bring your belongings from your house. Till tomorrow you will get your clothes. As of now, adjust with this." He came in front of me and handed me his clothes and talked softly after listening to me. What is wrong with him. At one time he is very angry another time he is talking softly as if nothing happened. He is bipolar.

"Thank you" I took his clothes without arguing as I don't have anything to wear. It is better than this wedding saree.

I went directly to my room which does not have anything. No bed nor furniture. I went into the bathroom with his clothes and freshened up after brushing my teeth. As I looked into the mirror his finger print marks were on my cheek lightly and my lip was slightly bleeding.I did not care as I don't have time. After Freshening up I feel fresh as I have looked into the mirror.

My hair has not dried yet and I wore his clothes with my previous inner wear. As it is an adjustable track no problem was there as I am very thin. I folded the track till above my feet as it is very long. The shirt is very loose for me but I think I can manage for today.

I went into the kitchen and started preparing for his breakfast. I don't know where they kept all the ingredients and utensils. It took some time to search for them but atlast I prepared a few rotis and aloo gravy. I served them on the dining table when he was descending downstairs.

"Serve the breakfast" he ordered me and stared for a long time without blinking once. I started serving him. Without glancing at me he started eating in silence. He glanced at her without noticing as I turned to bring a glass of water. He did not even speak a word after washing his hands and left for his office without turning.

Papa

Nikshitra's Pov:

I don't know what he is thinking without saying anything he left off. I don't even care now. I have so much work to complete. So I started cleaning the whole house. After one hour cleaning I started eating my breakfast as I don't even have energy because I did not ate anything after breakfast yesterday. Till my stomach was full I ate everything.

I started preparing lunch. Rice is cooked and brinjal curry is ready. Then I started doing the remaining house chores. In the afternoon 4 my works are completed. Then I started to eat my lunch sitting on the dining table seat. As I am tired , I wanted to rest so I slept in my room locking every door of the mansion.

"No...My father did not make any mistake. Please don't do anything to him. Please don't make my father homeless. If you want you can do anything to me but not my father. Ple..ase..." I begged him to leave my father. But he looked angry towards me as I don't know what my mistake is. I think he will beat me. I know this look. So I covered my face because of fear. I sat in front of him begging, weeping and sobbing continuously. He smirked at me but he had another plan in his mind. I was shivering as his hands were nearing me.

He was ready to hold me but I woke up scared looking around the surroundings and sweat broke up on my face. I got scared thinking of my dad. How is he? Has he eaten anything? This nightmare gave me fearful thoughts.

I dont have my mobile to call as it is in my dad's place. I have to call him to know about him. But how? I was in thoughts when I remembered there was a landline phone in the living room.

I ran hurriedly downstairs to check if the phone is working or not. To my luck it is working so I hurriedly called my dad. It was ringing but he did not lift, atlast when I was ready to hang up he lifted.

"Hello, Who is this speaking?" When I heard my dad's voice, tears gathered in my eyes. I cannot speak any word as my thoughts wandered to how I used to live happily with my dad. With no tensions in that small house. No one to scold, only happy life and happy memories. As I dont have my mother, he did not even bring up that topic to disappoint me as I am sensitive.

"Hello" My dad's voice rang in my ears as it brought me out of my reverie. Then I started speaking as he may cut the call.

"He...llo pa..papa", My voice became hoarse as I was crying continuously thinking about him.

"Hello Ni..kki, how are you beta? Are you fine? Is he treating you well? Have you eaten anything? I miss you very much beta. I am feeling very lonely here in this house without you. Hello are you there nikki ", I cried when my dad called my name, I remembered how he used to call me by my nickname which he kept very lovingly. With his continuous questions I know he cares for me so much. I know he is crying because I can hear from his voice. But I can't tell him anything as I know he will take all the blame on himself for my life.

"Papa how are you? I miss you so much and I am fine. Don't cry papa as I know you can manage everything there. I will come to meet you very soon papa. Dont worry. I also feel lonely without you. I am sorry I did not call you after coming back. I have eaten my lunch papa. Have you eaten? How did you prepare lunch papa as I know from the last 5 years I was preparing for you. Papa papa are you.." I spoke continuously as I was happy talking to my dad without any tension. He is my saviour. I can do anything for him as he is my life. In my 23 years of life he did not even once scold me.

"I made my lunch, don't worry about that as I have been cooking since you were born. But I forgot little things but it is no problem as I can manage. How is Ayush? Is he taking good care of you? If there is any problem, tell me. I will help you dont forget I am your dad" Asking about Ayush, my thoughts wandered to how he treated me. I wanted to tell everything to my dad as I was unhappy and scared of him. Today I did all the work to divert my mind as I can't accept that he slapped and said many awful things to me. I want to forget everything that he did to me.

"No dad, he is taking good care of me. He is very kind, and did not even let me do any work since I came here. Don't worry about me dad I am very happy here. Ayush is very nice to me. He speaks less but I know what he is thinking so no problem dad. He went to office as today there is an important meeting. He said if it is not important he will never goto the office on next day of the marriage. He apologised to me. So dont worry papa" I said to my dad covering my mouth to stop the sobs as I can't cry infront of him. If he knows that I am crying then he may get suspicious. So i covered it up not saying anything about Ayush as I don't know anything about his personal life. He may threaten my father if I will not obey him.

"Oh.. then I will speak to him tomorrow. Are you happy beta?" This one question which I do not want him to ask. Because I can't say any more lies to him. So I avoided it. But I cannot control my crying, So I covered my mouth with other hand. My legs turned numb by standing in one place I catched the sofa to stand properly.

"Papa the doorbell is ringing, I think he came. I will call you afterwards. Bye papa. Take care." I hung up the call as I can't lie to my dad. I lied again, I am sorry papa. I sat on the sofa weeping continuously with my head on my knees. My body was shaking as I was uncontrollable sobbing. But no one is there to console me. I don't want to tell lies to my papa. I never lied to him. I know I am doing a mistake by not telling him but I think it is better like this. As I cant burden him anymore.

After my crying session I got up and washed my face in my room. As it is dinner time I started to prepare the dinner. As I don't know when he will come. But I have to keep ready as he may get angry if not prepared.

By 9pm the dinner is ready. I was exhausted after doing all the work. So I laid down on the sofa. When I dozed off I don't know.

But some noise woke me up. As I got up half sleepy, squinting my eyes I saw a figure hovering over me. I got scared and pushed him off of me.

"How dare you push me?" He shouted, then I woke up completely. My widened eyes and mouth shows how shocked I am. Then I got up from the sofa standing and gave my hand to him to help him stand. But he glared at me and pushed my hand away from him. He got up by himself and muttered something under his breath.

"What?" I asked him, instead of answering me. He growled at me.

"Do you have any manners? Did you father not teach you anything? Who gave you permission to lie on my sofa. Why are you sleeping here? Have you prepared the dinner or not? " He asked many questions at one time. As I was not able to call him by his name.

"Devil" I muttered under my breath.

"What did you say", he shouted once again as I thought he heard.

"Nothing Sir. I prepared your dinner and did all my duties as you said Sir. You can check if you want SIR" I taunted him as I cannot bear his nonsense anymore.

Apology

Nikshitra's Pov:

I ignored him, and walked away to the kitchen. I don't want to talk to him thinking of how he threatened me with my father's job. He knows I will do anything for my dad, so he made the plan. If he thinks I cannot talk back to him then he is completely wrong. I felt bad when he called me slut and whore. But I have to give this marriage a chance, As I don't have any choice.

I will do the housework as it is my duty. But he cannot order me like he wants.

"Wait" His loud voice boomed in the mansion, I slightly flinched without turning to him rooted in my position.

"Have you called your dad today?" How does he know I called my dad. There is no one except me in the house. Is he stalking me? Are there any CCTV cameras here? I looked at the surroundings frantically with my widened eyes. I spotted one in the living room. Then I concluded that he is checking my every activity from morning to night. Is there any CCTV in my room?

I forgot to answer and avoided it after coming from my reverie.

"Are you deaf? I asked you, have you called your dad today? Speak it damnit? Yes or No?" He was inches away from me, I don't know when he walked to me this fast. His breathing is ragged, he is angry as I can feel it. I stared towards the floor. Will he slap me again? If I say yes or no I will get scolded. So I will tell the truth only.

"Ye..Yes, I am so..rry. I was missing him So I called him from the landline." I stuttered due to fear of him as I don't know what he will do. With unshed tears I stared at his eyes.

"How dare you call him. From tomorrow onwards you cannot call anybody, not even your dad. Is that clear?" He shouted at the end, I flinched when he held my shoulders tightly with both his hands leaving his marks.

"NO, YOU LISTEN TO ME. I am not your puppet. You cannot control my life however you want. I really did not think you could stalk me. You are so cheap. How can you think I will listen to you after what you have done. I will talk to my dad. I will meet him. What will you do? Huh? Will you fire him from his job? Then fire him, I don't care but I cannot live without talking to my dad. He has no one except me. How do you know? You have no emotions. You are heartless. You don't know what dad and mom means to children. As you don't have one." I shouted and left from there without caring how much my words hurt him. I was very angry as I don't know what came over me, I spoke to him rudely.

I hurriedly ran upstairs towards my room and locked the door. As I was unable to control my tears, it started flowing tremendously. I sat down on the floor hugging my knees, keeping my head in between sobbing continuously. I dozed off while sobbing as I am tired.

When I got up it was already late as I can see the time when I went downstairs after brushing and washing my puffy face due to continuous crying. As I dont have my clothes with me I wanted to ask him but my mind did not accept whether to ask him or not. So when I entered the kitchen it was 9 am. My stomach is grumbling. So I started to prepare breakfast. I was ready to take all the ingredients to make breakfast when someone knocked on the main door.

I opened the door slightly as I am afraid of who is there outside as I know Ayush might have gone to his office early because of yesterday's drama. I remembered he said he wants his breakfast ready till 8:30 am as he will leave for his office at 8:45am.

"Good morning Ma'am. Sir asked to deliver your clothes. Where should I keep it maam?" He politely asked me and I was happy seeing my belongings and opened the door wide, giving the space to enter. He might be 60 years old as he is in driver dress. I remembered when Ayush said he will send the driver to bring my belongings from my house.

"Goodmorning kaka, leave it here I will take it from here." I smiled and answered him politely. Looking at him, I thought of my dad. Sadness appeared on my face. But I changed my expression and asked him about Ayush.

"Kaka, have you seen Ayush going to the office in the morning? I think he did not eat anything. Will you send the breakfast to his office?" I requested him and g

He smiled gently towards me and accepted my request gladly.

"He went to the office early in the morning. I think he is upset because of something. As I have known him from childhood he rarely behaves like this. He never shows his emotions. But today he is not like everyday. I don't know what happened to him" he said and I was feeling very bad after remembering what I said to him yesterday in anger. I know I was angry when I spoke like that. But I know it is my mistake as I don't have any right to say that to anyone like that. I have to apologise. But how will I?

Then I got an idea to prepare his breakfast and send a sorry letter to him.

I hurriedly made 3 Dosa. I prepared the batter yesterday itself. I made chutney and packed the tiffin with a small note written sorry on it. I made the kaka wait but I gave the packed box to him and said thank you.

He blessed me and waved me bye.

I am nervous of what he will think, if he sees the note. Will he accept my apology?

I am nervous of what he will think, if he sees the note. Will he accept my apologies?

With his thoughts in my mind, I prepared my dosa and ate afterwards. Then I took my suitcase to my room and checked whether all my sufficient clothes were there or not. I checked my other suitcase also to see my files and certificates. I wanted to do a job. But I know it will be a dream that will never come true.

Sameer

Ayush Pov:

When I saw her in my white shirt, my mouth hung open. She is looking breathtaking and it was transparent so I can see her through the shirt. I became hard just seeing her. I don't know what I will do if she wears any revealing clothes. I can't control myself then. I want to have my way with her on the dining table so I avoid looking at her as she can guess what is running in my mind as she sees my eyes so I have to be careful. My eyes are always searching for her if she is not in front of me.

But I have to control my emotions as there is so much for me to get revenge from her. She has to regret it till she dies. I did not even speak a word at the dining table as I was preparing myself to become cold in front of her. She cannot see my true emotions. I have to be careful while planning against her as she can go away from me. So I did not scold her as she asked me for the clothes. She has to trust me first then I can break her however I want. She cooked delicious food. I wanted to praise her food but I kept it to myself. I think she has magic hands.

I remembered my mother,she cooked for me daily. She used to cook all my favourites whenever I wanted.

I want to say bye to her but I thought she may doubt my intentions as I slapped her earlier. I have to remain aloof. I cannot beat her. I have to control my temper. I think mental pain is stronger than physical pain. So I will break her trust when she falls for me. When I went to the office, everything was the same.

"Hello, Kaka. Good morning. Bring the clothes from the address I have sent you and deliver it to home as soon as possible" I called my driver to pick the clothes from her house.

"Sir these are the files you asked me to check and I have corrected it. Please check once then I will send it to the client" My secretary knocked on my door and gave the files to me to check if there is any mistake.

"It is Ok Mythri. I will check within an hour. I will send you the details of Mehra project details through the mail. Prepare the presentation till tomorrow morning then I will check if any improvements are needed or not. If any meeting is there it means postpone it as I am really tired" I told my secretary who smiled towards me. Like a friendly gesture but I remain aloof. I know she is not like other women who throw themselves at others. She was happily married 5 years ago and blessed with two children, one boy and one girl. She is like an elder sister to me. I dismissed her and got into my work.

As no one knows about my marriage there will be no commotion. I don't want to reveal my marriage news in front of anybody as it is revenge. I will make her mine in all ways then break her beyond repair. So she will never think of betraying others.

"Hello buddy, what are you doing? Work work.... What will you gain by working so much other than money" Sameer barged into my room without knocking and taunted me about my work. But I didn't care as he was like that only.

"Peace" I said one word and again started doing my work without glancing at him again.

"After the first day of marriage, why did you come to the office? You are behaving as if you did not do anything last night. Are you still a virgin buddy? Don't tell me I can't listen" The drama queen appeared again. With a bored expression I glanced at him and showed him my middle finger. Then also he did not budge. He was shocked as nothing happened yesterday. He does not know the main reason why I married her. I made up a cooked up story and he believed it like her father.

"What do you want Sameer? If you are here to disturb me then get out." I shouted at him but he was not ready to leave.

"One question buddy. Just one please. Yesterday nothing happened?" He requested with his puppy face so I gave my answer in a no.

" I thought my friend will atlast lose his virginity at 26 years. But what I got as an answer. No. Are you an idiot? She is your wife, you have rights to claim her. But who am I talking to. THE MR. AYUSH KHURANA. I cannot change you. I am not a saint like you." What is wrong with them. If I am a virgin what is the problem? I know what my mother taught me. She said never ever lose the precious because of your past mistakes. I was following my mother words what is wrong in that.

"As she is new to this relationship. I think she takes time to get close. We both need some time to understand each other. I also need some space. So it is better like this. So don't put your shitty ideas into my brain" I convincingly explained to him the situation so he would believe it without asking any further questions.

"Ok Sorry buddy. I thought... It's ok. I will leave for now. I know she is not your type of girl so I thought she trapped you. But I think you may be happy with her if you like her. You deserve every happiness in this world my friend. All the best and Bye." He left, leaving me in regret. I know he will oppose the idea of revenge so I did not tell anything to him. I know when time comes I have to tell him. Whether he will forgive me or not. I don't know. But I don't have any option other than this marriage.

As I was in the office working, I watched what she was doing at home as I had installed CCTV cameras everywhere in the house except my bedroom. She was working all day I think so as she is sleeping looking tired. As I was ready to off the camera I saw her descending downstairs hurriedly. I was thinking about what happened when I saw her dialing a number from the landline. I forgot to disconnect the phone. It is better as I will know who she is talking to. When she was speaking I called my security and told them to check the call details and told them to record the call on my landline. They forwarded the details within a minute and relief washed over me as it was her father who she was speaking to. I have to listen to the conversation about what she is saying as she will hang up after sometime. I was very tired of the work. From morning I am attending back to back meetings without any break. I didn't even do my lunch.

When I am free I check the files which are pending. After listening to the conversation I felt bad but I think my plan is working. She will not say anything about me to her dad as she loves her dad so much.

When I entered the house at midnight. It was pitch dark and the door was locked so I opened it with my key. When I thought no one was there in the hall I caught a figure who is sleeping on the sofa without any fear of outer world. She looked in peace. I was staring at her continuously and traced her forehead with my fingers as I couldn't stop myself standing in front of the sofa. When she wiggled I got out of my trance and removed my hand from her face and was ready to get out from there but my leg got hit by the teapoy then I fell on her. Then she pushed me with her hands as I was very close to her, chest to chest touching, breaths mingling and staring at each other.

Then she spoke the words which hurt my soul. I know it was my mistake but my ego is bigger than her. I beared her with taunts and everything. I asked the question which is roaming in my mind as if she will answer the truth or not. After a lot of threatening she said she called her dad.

If she calls him again then she may spill the truth so I have to take care from the beginning only. So I restricted her from calling her dad or anyone.

Then she spoke hurtful words towards me. I was deeply hurt when she said about my parents. As I cannot show my emotions in front of her I stood motionless. Tears started gathering in my eyes. To avoid the situation I have maintained a cold expression without giving any hint to her.

I am controlling my anger as If I will burst on her or worse beat her. So I tightened my fists and clenched my jaw to control my rising temper. I want to beat the shit out of her as how can she say about my parents. She does not have any right to say anything about them. She doesn't even belong here in this high class society. She has no standards. I want to slap her then and there. But to execute my plan I have to bear this.

I did not even sleep a wink last night as her words kept running in my mind. So I went jogging to refresh my mind. I left for the office early in the morning as I didn't want to see her face. I don't want to remember the moment when she said those hurtful words.

"Sir, your breakfast. Driver Kaka delivered at the lobby" Mytri knocked on my door and gave the box to me. I thought who had sent it then she said as if reading my thoughts.

Then I opened the box to get a surprise. As the first box of the carriage has only white chit neatly folded. I unfolded the chit and saw what was written in it.

"Sorry" Automatically a smile formed on my face when I saw the emoticon. She drew it. With two hands on her ears and lips pouting. I smiled seeing the drawing.

Then I opened the other box and saw dosa. It is my favourite as my mom used to make it so many times for me. My memories came back when we used to be a happy family without sadness.

I ate everything with a smile on my face. It is delicious. Her hands do magic. But I have to praise her for cooking this much delicious food.

---Authors note

Long chapters ahead guys. It will be more interesting afterwards. So please vote and comment.

Hug and Kiss

Ayush Pov:

With a smile on my face I entered the house in the evening at 7pm. It feels like home now as she is living in my house.

It was dark so I switched on the lights. I was searching for her but she is nowhere to be seen. I think she is in her room. I went directly to my room to freshen up. Today I was not tired like I usually do. No one wrote any letter for me. It is my first time recieving a sorry note from someone. All are scared to face me other than Sameer.

"Tomorrow, be ready at 9 am." I said to her when she entered my bedroom without making any noise. She did not know that I was watching her from the mirror as she was facing my back.

"Why? Where are we going? Don't tell me You want to leave me? I know it is your decision, If you want you can leave me but don't say anything to my Papa."She asked nonchalantly without remembering the previous incident. I got angry when she spoke about leaving me. I turned towards her while combing my hair. I strode towards her but she moved backwards, as she hit the wall I grabbed her shoulders.

"You cannot leave me. You will live forever with me. Is that clear? If you speak once again about leaving me, then you will face the horrible consequences which you never even imagined in your life. Remember that you have a father." I threatened her with my glaring eyes, tightly clenched fists. I have to be calm. I repeated in my mind several times to evaporate my anger.

"Where do you want to take me then?" With her shocked filled gaze she asked me slowly, fear creeping up her body as sweat beads broke on her forehead. I moved her side locks from her face behind her ear slowly with my one hand. I gazed at her eyes which shone brightly before our marriage and now some deep emotions like hurt.

"We are going to your fathers house tomorrow. I will inform your dad about coming to the house. So be prepared and behave yourself. If I know that you have said anything about us then you will know what I will do." Her face lightened after hearing about going to her fathers house. She smiled and grinned at me. As if not believing my words she asked once again.

"Really? Are you telling the truth?" I nodded in confirmation then she suddenly hugged me tightly, her both hands under my arms at the back, her head resting on my heart. I am shocked. I can see that she is very much happy. She is grinning.

"Thank you so much, devil, " she said, hiding her face in my chest not realizing what she is doing to me. I slowly wrapped my both arms around her back. One on her waist and another on her back. I can feel her touch through the fabric. I was feeling her body with my hands and rested my chin on her forehead as she is so small in front of me.

"I forgive you" I calmly said and watched her reaction. She immediately left my hold realizing her position. I missed her presence in my arms. She widened her eyes in realization as a red hue appeared on her cheeks, I chuckled. I have seen her fidgeting in her place feeling awkward about the hug, eyes cast downwards, murmuring incoherent words. I bought her out of dreamland by startling her with my voice.

"Sorry, I got carried away. I am really sorry about yesterday, I didn't mean it that way. I was not thinking at that time as I was angry at you. It was my mistake. How can I bring up your parents when it is not their fault as it is your fault" I glared at her for what she said. When she saw me glaring, then she realized what she said. Eyes widened, mouth open close then she closed her mouth shut with her both hands.

"Oh my God Oh my God. I am an idiot. Now he will not spare me. What will I do? I will run from here, it is the better option than to face the devil in anger" She talked to herself without realizing she was speaking out loud.

"Stop Right There" I growled angrily and walked towards her fast. I grabbed her arm tightly with my one hand when she tried to run away.

"No No I am sorry. You are very good. I am bad. Please let me go. I will keep my mouth shut. I don't know what I am saying. Please let me go once. I will never ask anything from you. Ple...ase " She blabbered continuously with a cute pout on her face, eyes staring directly at me without fear, nose scrunched and lips pouting. My anger flew away just by seeing her pout. Then and there I want to kiss her lips which are inviting me to devour her. My heart started beating more than normal against my rib cage. I held her neck softly with my other hand without letting her go.

I leaned forward to kiss her, at the same time she realized what I was going to do so she moved her face to the right side in a blink. My lips landed on the left cheek. She stood there shocked and I started kissing her cheek. I started peppering small pecks on the left side of her cheek without removing my tight hold on her. With my eyes closed I inhaled her scent and started going downwards to her jaw to kiss her more. My hold on her neck became more tight. I wanted to bite her soft round puffy cheek once. I peppered small kisses wetting her skin with my lips. I rolled my tongue over my lips to moist them. I bite on her cheek lightly with my teeth.

"Ahhhh" she screamed in pain when I bit her, then she opened her eyes slowly turning towards me. Her dark eyes showed desire for me. I am feeling content seeing her in my arms breathing heavily, eyes closed holding my shoulders with her both hands. I feel different emotions when I am with her. I want to hold her, kiss her, sleep with her.

She gently removed her hands from my shoulders, I felt the warmness subsided from my skin. Her touch gave me warmth. She stumbled a bit after I removed my hold from her body. I was there ready to hold her but she managed herself by showing her right palm in front of me.

"Stop, I will manage myself." Tears gathered in her eyes. Then she left from there without turning backwards.

I have to control myself before I do anything that I regret. Why can't I control myself when she is in front of me? I sat on the bed thinking about my previous actions holding my head with both hands. I felt so good while kissing her. I never wanted to stop kissing her. I want to claim her as mine. I will become a puppet when she is so close to me. My anger calms down when I see her smiling face. I have to remember to get my revenge before getting attracted to her.

Meeting Her Father

Nikshitra's Pov:

How can I allow him to kiss me? What will he think of me? He thinks I am desperate for him. No, I am not like that. I have to avoid him. I was happy when he said to meet my father. I cannot control my happiness at that time. I thought he would not allow me to meet him. But I was wrong.

My heart is racing so fast. I am shivering thinking about his closeness. I felt good when he kissed me on my face. No one ever kissed me like that. I was giggling thinking about that but I know he can never change. My tears apparently followed for what will happen if it is acting.

I think he changed. I have to trust him. If not, why will he allow me to meet my father? And also he is coming with me. What will he gain if he is acting? I have to give him one chance to gain my trust.

I laid down on the floor with a bedsheet and a pillow under my face. I covered myself with a thin blanket which I got from another room when I was cleaning. I will meet my dad tomorrow. I am so happy. What will I say to him if he asks me how I am? I will talk with him tomorrow. I cannot say anything about Ayush. He will get heartbroken if he gets any idea about my relationship. I have to manage this.

I woke up early in the morning because I was happy to see my dad. I was doing every work happily smiling to myself. I want to wake him up at 7am. But I don't think it will be a good idea. If he gets angry we will not go to my dad's house. So I rejected that idea and prepared breakfast.

"Oh.. oh... You are looking happy." He came down at 7:30 am, folding his arms and flexing his muscles. He is looking handsome with his bed hair and white t shirt and black track. I realized I was staring at him continuously. I got awkward remembering yesterday night's events.

"Uh ..Uh I was wa.s. No.. Nothing. Breakfast is ready. Come and eat. I will arrange it on the dining table in a few minutes." I said to him to avoid the awkward tension running between us. He smirked realizing I was gawking at him.

"I will freshen up and come. Till then you arrange it." He calmly said to me and went upstairs to his room.

"Come and join me as it is already late." I was shocked when he said to eat with him. I was afraid whether he would scold me if I sat on the dining chair with him. But he did not even lift his head while eating. So it became easy for me to eat my food.

We silently ate breakfast and got ready to go to my dad's house. He locked the main door. He was walking fast towards his car. I was following him silently, staring at his back. When he opened his car door and sat in the driver seat. I was wondering whether I should sit in the passenger seat or not. I slowly walked to the passenger side and opened the door and sat silently without looking at him.

He started driving and I glanced at him without him noticing. He is so handsome with his glasses on. Short stubble growing on his sharp jaw. Straight nose and pink lips which were on me yesterday. I am grinning thinking about it. Red hue covered my cheeks and I shied away from him. I turned my face towards the window.

"What are you thinking. Don't stare at me like that. I know I am handsome. Remember you have to not say anything about our relation to your dad. If you say anything then you will bear the consequences" He smirked at the end of his sentence as he knows I don't have any choice than to obey him.

"Ok I will not say anything as I know my dad will be guilty if I am not happy with you. I will never say anything to him about us till I die. You can be happy without tension as I will never say it. So please dont blackmail me." I taunted him at last as I was feeling angry towards him. But he neglected my taunt and was silent throughout the drive.

The car stopped near my house which is in a local community. I directly got down without waiting for him and ran fast to the main door and rang the doorbell. When the door opened I saw my father standing with a grin on his face as he saw me. I hugged him tightly without giving a chance to speak a word.

"I miss you so much papa. How are you? Are you eating your food on time or not? Are you taking your BP tablets regularly? If you are not taking means I will call the doctor Uncle and complain to him about you" I spoke without leaving my hold on him. My dad smiled looking at me. Tears gathered in his eyes and one tear left from his left eye. He left my hold and gathered my face in his both hands. My dad was looking at me with so much affection as we were not separated anytime in our life. It is the first time when we were this much longer without each other.

"I am good Nikki. How are you? I miss you too, my bachha. Come inside first then we'll talk " My dad said as we were in front of the door only. I did not notice when Ayush came beside me as he was staring at me with different emotions in his eyes.

"Ayush How are you beta? I am sorry I forgot to let you inside. Please come inside." My dad greeted my husband. It is feeling different as I think he is my husband. Ayush took the blessing of my dad and greeted smilingly without giving any doubt.

"I am fine Uncle. I was busy with my office work so that's why we were late to meet you. I am sorry Uncle if not I have come to meet you after marriage day only. However, how is your health Uncle? Are you taking your medicines properly or not?" He genuinely asked my dad about his health as I can see it in his eyes whether he is speaking truth or lies. He is smiling speaking to my dad.

"It's Ok beta. It is not a problem. Nikki has called me and said you were busy. So it is not at all a problem for me. Is she behaving well with you? If not I will explain to her. She will definitely listen to me.

So dont worry." My dad asked him and Ayush fidgeted in his place where he is seated on the sofa beside me. He was feeling awkward fists clenched tight and staring down with his clenched jaw. I was worried whether he would complain about me to my father.

"Nothing Uncle. She is really good. No problem with her as she is taking care of me like a baby. I will be forever grateful to you for accepting this marriage. She made my life perfect. Without her I don't know what my life will become." He changed his expression looking emotionally at me, holding my right hand with his left hand. I was happy when he praised me but I dont know these were all lies to trap me in his revenge.

We ate our lunch speaking animatedly with each other. As time went by, we were ready to leave at 7pm. But I don't want to leave my dad yet. I want to convince Ayush to be here today and we can go tomorrow morning as it is Sunday today.

"Ayush beta can you stay here today? I miss my Nikki. Tomorrow you can go after breakfast. I did not leave her for a single day before marriage" My dad requested both of us to stay till the last minute. As I don't have any say in it I did not convince Ayush.

So Ayush gave in and made some calls to his office as he will be late tomorrow morning. I was very happy as I can be in my home today. I can sleep on my bed today. But I forgot that we both have to sleep on my single bed. We don't have any extra rooms as it is a double bed room house. I realized when we both entered my room following him behind me.

He was looking at my room keenly watching every wall which had pictures of me from small till I grew up. It has my dad in every picture with me.

"So cute" he whispered and smiled seeing my photo frame. I was a toddler licking my thumb in my mouth with a cute pink dress and pink woolen hat grinning showing my two front teeth. I was very chubby and cute when I was small.

After realizing what he said he changed into a blank expression and turned towards me while I was mesmerizing him when he was giving a compliment to me. I was grinning from ear to ear. Then he turned towards the bed.

"Is there any other room to sleep? We cannot adjust in this single room." He asked me the question which I was afraid of. I cannot let him walk out of this room. If my dad sees he will get suspicious.

"No, You can sleep on the bed and I will sleep on the floor, as I can manage. I will bring my dad's clothes so you can change and sleep on the bed." I directly left from there to avoid any conversation to bring my dad clothes.

"Here, take it and change. We don't have other clothes better than this. So adjust for today. Till then I will arrange the bed for you" He went to the attached bathroom in my room without any complaint taking the clothes.

When he came out he was looking cute in white kurta. I want to pinch his cheeks to look this adorable with a confused expression as it is loose for him. I arranged my bed on the floor with one pillow above it.

"If you want anything ask me?" I questioned him as he wanted to ask something. But he did not open his mouth so I took my nightwear which was there as extra and went to the bathroom to change from my saree.

I came out and saw that my bed on the floor is removed and the pillow is arranged on the cot. I was ready to ask why he did it? Before that he answered my question.

"I don't want to create any doubt for your father. If he sees it then we will have to explain. So it is better if you sleep on the bed with me." My mouth hung open. He did not give me a chance to speak for once. As I don't have any option I got on one side of the bed and laid hugging myself turning backwards to him. The bed dipped from the other side and his hand was touching my back. It is very small for two people in this single bed. He is very close to me. I can hear his shallow breaths near my ear. There is no gap between us. I can feel that.

A hand came near my waist. I was frightened when he touched me through my clothes. I gasped and my eyes widened and I closed my mouth with both hands to not make any sound. He cannot know I am awake. If he knows I don't know what he will do to me.

"Don't act. I know you are not sleeping . Look at me."I did not budge from my place and acted like I was sleeping.

"Ah..What are you doing?" He pinched me on my waist when I didn't answer him. I turned towards him angrily and shifted closer as there was no place for me. If not I will fall down.

He was staring at me longingly then he did the unexpected to which I was shocked.

---Authors Note

I will try to update alternate days. Please bear with me. If you like my story please vote and comment. I am Sorry if any grammatical errors are there.

Unexpected Kiss

Ayush Pov:

"What are you doing to me? Why can't I resist you? Are you feeling the same Nikki?" My heartbeat is racing fast, also I can hear her breathing fast. She is very close to me, there is no gap between us. I was holding her in my arms, keeping my both hands on either side of her waist. I want to touch her every inch of her body. I want to touch every part of her body with my hands and lips.

"What did you say?" She whispered slowly, staring in my eyes. Her heartbeat is racing the same as mine. I can feel sweat on her forehead and on her body. She is slightly shivering wherever I touch her. She is feeling hot.

"What did I say? I did not said anything. I asked what are you doing to me? That's it", I know what she wants to ask but I want to avoid it so I acted as if I did not call her name. I never called her name in front of her, it is the first time. Her name rolled of my tongue very smoothly. When I call her name I feel she belongs to me. No one belongs to me in this world. But I felt connected towards her.

"I know you are telling lies. I heard correctly. You called my name. It is the first time you called me by my name. Please, I want to hear it. Call me Nikki once", She requested pouting cutely with her nose scrunched upwards and eyes staring downwards avoiding staring directly at me.

"What will you do If I call your name? Tell me any suggestions, if it is ok for me then I will proceed with it. Otherwise you should give me what I want. Is it ok with you?" I smirked looking at her. Her mouth opened and eyes glaring at me when I gave that suggestion. I know what she is thinking, she is thinking correctly about me. I want her to kiss me. So I gave this idea.

"No need to call me by my name. It is ok for me. You will only call me one day. It is a waste of time to argue with you." She swiftly turned towards the other side leaving my shoulders which were held by her both hands.

"NIKKI", I held her in one hand and turned her towards me. She hit my head directly at a sudden collision, noses touching, lips with an inch gap. I said her name and our lips met at the same time. I wanted to kiss her for so long. I pecked her lips barely touching them. Then I leaned forward holding her neck with my one hand and another holding her waist. It was my first kiss. I never kissed any girl in my life. My breathing became shallow, the same as hers. She gasped and opened her eyes widely with shock written all over her face.

I pecked her once lightly with both my upper lip and lower lip touching her lips. I lightly moved my face to angle her lips. I bent her body downwards as we are both sidewards. I did not leave her lips angling her face. I started pressing my lips more tightly towards her lips. I started moving my lips slowly. Then I opened my mouth and traced her upper lip with my tongue and did the same with her lower lip while I traced her body with my one hand through her clothes. I slowly crept my fingers under her tshirt and started tracing her bare waist with my hand while kissing her. It feels so soft, warm and smooth.It feels so divine. She shivered slightly when I touched her bare but she did not object so I proceeded to wander my hand around her stomach. When I touched her belly button she stopped with her hand holding mine and moved away from my lips which were ready to devour her. I want to kiss her one more time but I know she is feeling shy as I can see her ears and cheeks turned red, eyes casting downwards not meeting my eyes at least once. She abruptly got up from the bed breathing heavily and ran to the bathroom not even looking at me once.

After a few minutes she came, took a pillow from the bed and bedsheet from the cupboard, arranged it neatly on the floor and slept there itself without bothering me. She totally avoided looking at me. I want to talk to her but I don't know what to say. It is getting awkward for me. I scratched my neck twice and I was feeling shy. I grabbed another pillow and hugged tightly covering my face with it and turned to the opposite side of her. I slept thinking about the kiss, grinning lightly with a smile on my face. I am getting attracted towards her.

When I woke up in the morning Nikshitra was not there in the bedroom. I saw the time, it was 7am I got up from the bed and went to the bathroom to brush my teeth. I was wiping my face with the towel when I saw her entering the room. She was shocked at first but regained her posture.

"Come for breakfast. Papa is waiting for you." She said without even meeting my eyes and ran away from the room. I was staring where she was standing before. I smirked seeing in her direction at how she is behaving with me. It is only starting. From now onwards I will break you more. You wait and watch Nikshitra. You will regret living in this world. When you start loving me I will break you beyond repair. You cannot trust anybody in this life, I will see to it when I leave you.

"Thank you for coming beta and whenever you are free, feel free to come here. From now onwards call me papa same as Nikki. Take care of my child. If she does anything wrong, tell me. I will explain to her." We ate breakfast and left for my house. Her dad said thanks but I don't care as it will be over within a few years.

"Bye Papa. I will take care of her. It is not a problem Papa if she does anything wrong as she is my responsibility. Dont worry and take care of yourself", To gain their trust I have to act, So I smiled and said bye to her dad holding her hand in mine.

I left from there driving rashly to my mansion without glancing at her, not even speaking a word with her.

"Get down" I said harshly and she got down seeing my face for one last time. I was angry at myself for behaving like that with her. I have kissed her. How can I kiss her? I have started to feel for her. I have to stop getting closer to her.

I fastly drove to my office thinking about the past which made my life like this. I was happy in my life but one girl destroyed everything.

I entered my office without greeting the staff who was terrified looking at me as I strode fast and sat in my chair controlling my anger. I saw the family photo which is present on my desk and slightly traced it with my fingers and tears escaped my eyes. My anger evaporated looking at the picture. In my 27 years of life I never felt both feelings at the same time, like and hatred towards one person.

Whenever I see Nikki, she makes me feel addicted towards her.S he has average looks with plumpy cheeks, captivating eyes and slim body. Her actions brought me closer to her. I have not to fall for her looks which are deceiving.

Sometimes she gets feisty and next minute scared. Her eyes which held so many emotions speak more than her words of what she is feeling. She does unexpected things when she is happy. When she hugged me I felt content and warm. I have to be strict towards her, after this drama completes.--Authors note

Thank you readers. Please vote and comment if you like my story.

Accident

Nikshitra's Pov:

I don't know what his problem is. One time he behaved well with me and another minute became harsh. I don't know what runs in his mind. I have to prepare myself for the worst. I conclude that he is bipolar. He has several mood swings but I am happy that he behaved very nice with my dad. My dad can't get any doubt if I am not happy as I don't want to burden him anymore.

Remembering last night's events I can't forget what he did. He called my name for first time. Thinking about that a smile formed on my face. He freaking KISSED me yesterday. He stole my first kiss, but I never regret it as he is my husband. Why? How? I don't know. I was scared at that time but I can't refuse him. Whenever he looks at me longingly I can't resist him. I cant remove that from my mind. Why he kissed me? He insulted me with bad names then why he kissed me? I have to be careful as it is moving fast. I Have to keep my emotions in check whenever he is around me. But I felt on top of the world when he kissed me on my lips. I can say that I am his first kiss as he doesn't know how to kiss the same as me. I was grinning thinking about that and feeling shy.

I was working in the kitchen preparing lunch for me as he was not there. He was super angry when he dropped me at the house. I don't know the reason so I neglected. When he feels like telling me, he will tell me either in anger or when he trusts me. It takes time to develop trust so I have a life long time to wait for him. I am confused as of now as he behaves good and bad with me. I don't trust him as of now but I feel different kinds of emotions whenever he is around me.

I prepared aloo curry with rice. I ate late as I was not feeling hungry and completed my other chores doing laundry, mopping, etc.

"Hello Papa" I called my dad in the evening and spoke to him for some time.

"Hello Nikki, You did not call me after reaching home", I brought my mobile with me while leaving from my home as I was bored without that. Ayush doesn't know that I brought my mobile with me. When I called my dad without knowing, he was angry with me. I have to talk to my dad to know about his health. It is very important to me.

"Sorry Papa. I forgot to inform you as I was busy doing work. Have you been doing well? Have you eaten?" I asked, thinking about how he will manage without me. I am worried as I am not there with him.

"Today morning only you have seen me Nikki. Don't take any tension about me. I am very happy as you are happy. Please take care of yourself and take care of Son in law. I am getting an office call. I will call you after sometime. Is it ok?" I cut the call saying Ok. I was feeling bored so I sat on the sofa cross legged scrolling Instagram feed on my mobile. I passed the time by one hour in the evening. I was feeling droopy so I went to my room and slept.

"Ah..." When the landline phone rang from downstairs I hurriedly woke up and ran down the stairs fastly, but in hurry I slipped one step and fell down rolling my body. My body collapsed on the ground near the last step. I was feeling pain on my forehead, right leg and left hand. The pain was unbearable as I screamed for help.

"Papa.. Ah..Ah.. please somebody help me" I tried to get up with my one hand holding the ground. The tears started flowing due to the pain. But I was determined to get up, but my right leg is not moving and I have tried to bend my leg towards my knees but it is very much painful to move even an inch. I think I sprained my leg. My forehead is slightly bleeding on the right side. I touched it with my right hand as I cant lift my left hand as it has scratches near my elbow. Where I touched it stings and blood can be seen in my hand.

"Ay..ush. please help me. Come fast." I was thinking about him and calling him as I fall down again unable to bear the pain. I forgot to bring my mobile with me. How can I be careless? That's Why papa says to be careful but I do not listen to him. As I am unable to move anymore, crying helplessly, sobbing to myself I don't know when I lost consciousness.

When I woke up I was seeing the surroundings squinting my eyes. When I tried to lift my left hand it pained me so much that I laid down without moving my body. I was in Ayush's room as I could see his dark walls around me and his soft mattress where I first came. My hand, leg and forehead are covered with bandages as I can see them. I tried to touch my forehead with my right hand but it was slightly painful when I touched it.

"Nikki, When you woke up? You should have called me? How are you feeling now? Is it painful?" He entered from the balcony door. I think he was speaking to someone as he kept his mobile to his ear. He hung up seeing me waking up from the bed. I can see worry lines on his forehead. He was worried about me. I can see it in his eyes. His eyes are asking several questions and I can feel the tension from his words.

"I am fine Ayush. My hands and legs are in pain. I can't move my body. I know you want to ask me how I fell down. I slipped from the stairs as I was not seeing when the phone rang. I ran fast and I got up at that time so I was sleepy. So here I am. Dont scold me now please. I am tired as I can't even move an inch. So please. Ha.. I forgot to ask what the doctor said? As I can see the bandages wrapped around my body." I asked directly without beating around the bush.I want to divert his mind so I can't hear him scolding 'how careless I am'. I was not successful with it.

"How can you not see? Are you that dumb? You have to be careful while descending the stairs. Are you a child? How can you be so careless? What if something major happens to you? What will I answer to your dad?" He shouted at me for being careless. I can see that he is very much tense and worried so I kept my mouth shut, staring downwards avoiding his eyes. As I cant lift my body nor move anywhere, I laid down seeing the other side.

"Look at me NIKKI when I am speaking to you. If I was late for another hour what would have happened to you. When you bring your mobile with you, why can't you use it? Don't say that I was in a hurry, I forgot. Now onwards you will not move from this bed as the doctor said your ankle is sprained. It takes one week to heal your complete wounds. You will take rest. Other than going to washroom you cannot get up from this bed. Is that clear?" He scolded and shouted loudly at me. How did he know that I brought my mobile with me? But I was feeling happy as he cared about me for the first time. He was showing his true emotion so I am feeling so much happy in my heart. My heart is racing fast hearing his worry in his voice. So I nodded only as I didn't know what to answer him. If I say no he will shout. It is better to take his help as I can't do any work with this broken leg.

"Ok If you want anything Call me. I will call the maid to do the household chores and to take care of you when I am in office. If you need anything ask me. I will bring it." He calmed down and said to me. I was fisting my right hand and crushed my top tightly making it wrinkled. I want to goto bathroom now. How can I ask him? I am feeling embarrassed. I gathered some courage to ask him to help as I can't control anymore.

"Ayu..sh, Can you please take me to bathroom now?" I asked him, I closed my eyes as I am feeling embarrassed and shy to look in front of him. I gasped when he stood straight and lifted me up suddenly.

"Haaa.." I was shocked when he kept one hand under my both knees and another around my waist. I grabbed his neck tightly as I was afraid that I would fall down. He was looking at me without even blinking once. His touch made me feel tingles in my stomach. I remembered how close we were to each other yesterday night. I was feeling shy remembering that red colour formed on my cheeks. I can feel my body warm due to his touch.

He slowly walked till the bathroom door and opened it and got me down on the floor removing his hold from me. When I was unbalanced and ready to fall down he managed to catch me at the same time. I was frightened and closed my eyes to feel any pain in my body. I opened my eyes slowly as I could feel his hold on my waist and he held me tightly towards his body not letting me go.

"Let me go." I said and he came back from the trance as we both were staring at each other without blinking.

"Be careful." He said avoiding my gaze and removing his hand from my waist slowly. I came slowly from the washroom and opened the door lock after completing my work. He was waiting near the bathroom door thinking deeply, keeping his finger on his lip and one hand on his neck rubbing. He is looking very handsome. I know he is very tired as he came directly from the office directly. I didn't even ask if he had eaten or not. How careless of me I thought and slapped my forehead with my right hand.

"Haa... it hurts." I forgot that my forehead hurt. He turned towards me as he was facing backwards till now.

"What are you doing? I said I will help you. Why don't you listen to me for once? Who am I talking to." He said and lifted me bridal style without asking me. I have to get used to his touch. His sudden actions make me feel elated and surprised.

He put me down on the bed carefully and brought another from the other side and kept it under my leg. I liked this caring Ayush. I was grinning from ear to ear in my heart seeing this side of him.

"Have you eaten dinner? I forgot to ask you. I did not prepare it as you did not come early. If you want I will prepare." I asked him silently, whispering the last part to myself. The luck was not on my side as he was angry the next second glaring at my face to dare to speak another word.

"Will you prepare dinner for me with this condition. Are you out of your mind? I am not a sadist that I will make them work on who is sick. I will prepare dinner for now. From tomorrow the cook will do the work. Don't worry about it and now take a rest." He said and went out of the room growling to himself in anger.

---Authors Note

Thank you readers. I got 600 views. It is my first time writing a story. So please forgive me for any mistakes. Thank you once again for motivating me. Please if you like this story vote and comment

Care

Ayush Pov:

When I entered the house no one opened the door after knocking several times so I opened the lock with the spare keys which were with me. Once I opened no lights were on. It is dark so I switched on the lights walking slowly till switchboard. What I saw shocked me to the core. When I saw Nikki lying down I was numb for a second as I couldn't move my body from there. I panicked and ran fast to her and sat in front of her lying body. I picked her head and saw the bruise which was formed on her forehead and it was bleeding.

"Nikki...Nikki.. get up..Please get up Nikki. What happened to you? " I touched her forehead which was bleeding and took out my handkerchief from my pocket and pressed slightly on her forehead to stop the bleeding. My shivering hands touched her cold body to check any other wounds. I checked her breathing with my fingers keeping near her nose. I don't know why I was afraid. One tear escaped from my left eye seeing her in this condition. I felt bad when she was in this unresponsive state.

When she did not get conscious I carried her bridal style keeping my one hand under her legs and another on her waist. She was light weight and I felt like she did belong to me when I was carrying in my arms. My heart raced fast when her head touched near my heart. I can feel her cold body now as it is very close to me making me feel different emotions which I don't know.

I carried her to my bedroom and carefully laid her on the mattress keeping a pillow under her head. I took another cloth from my closet and removed the handkerchief which was full of blood. Then I tied the cloth on her forehead.

"Hello Dr. Bhatra, Ayush speaking here. Come fast to my house. It is urgent. No need for any explanations. Is that clear?" I calmly said to him but seeing him unresponsive to my call I got angry. How can he delay me? I was getting worried seeing her in this condition and this doctor is irritating me by not answering me. If he does not come I have to take her to the hospital without any delay. I can guess that she fell from the stairs. I don't even know if she has any major injuries from the fall.

"But Si..r, As of now I am bu..sy with another patient." He stammered afraid of my reaction. I got angry when he said he cannot come. So I have to deal with it my way. They will not listen when I request so I showed my real face to those who do not dare to speak against me.

"If you don't come in half an hour I will cancel your medical license. I will make your life hell. I will see to it. Be in my house in half an hour otherwise you will be on road in 24 hours." I threatened him and shouted loudly. I was very angry. I have to calm down. I fisted my hand tightly making my knuckles red and jaw tight and growled into the phone.

"Yes Si..r. I will come. Please don't do anything to me. I will be in half an hour." I think he got scared and I could hear his footsteps running. He knows if I threaten, I will not go backward and feel remorse towards them. I will make it happen.

I cut the call and came towards the bed where she was lying with her eyes closed. I took her right hand and touched it smoothly with my fingers. I was feeling good as I held her hand. I held her hand in between my both hands and rubbed to make it warm as it is cold. I was feeling her soft, smooth fingers with my hands. I took another and did the same to that. Then I slightly kissed her on the back of the hand. I do not want to remove my lips but I saw some scratches on the left elbow. I took some antiseptic cream from the first aid box, cleaned the blood and applied it gently. I was afraid if it stings her so I carefully applied it, blowing air on her wound while applying it. After tying the bandage around her I pecked her elbow with my lips. My warm lips touched her cold hand, I felt content closing my eyes feeling tears flow from my eyes.

"Nikki.. why are you doing this to me. Why do you make me feel like this? When I saw you lying there lifelessly. I felt like I died at that moment. Why don't you take care of yourself? If I met you in another situation I may fall in love with you. But I have to get revenge from you. You have to pay for it without leaving this world. I can only give you pain. Not anyone , nor you can harm yourself. I only have that right." I was talking to her animatedly and staring at her continuously, holding her hand in one hand and stroking her hair while sitting on the other side of the bed.

I am getting attracted to her. Whenever I am near her I want to touch her, kiss her. I don't want to move away from her when she is close to me. She is looking so beautiful with no makeup, only bindi between her eyebrows and plumpy cheeks which I want to bite everytime I see them. Her unmoving body made me feel like some part has been lost within me.

"She has to take rest for a week and cannot move from the bed. Her light leg has twisted so it will take time to heal. Give these medicines from time to time. No need to worry about your wife Sir." The doctor came within half an hour and checked her. He said that she got a sprain in ankle and some minor wounds on her left hand. He stopped the bleeding on her forehead and cleaned her wounds while I was watching. The doctor was watching Nikki as she wore a nuptial chain around her neck and he guessed that she is my wife. I don't like that look in his eyes so I glared at him giving him a daring look to speak another word after that. He went out after giving the prescription.

"Thank you Dr. Bhatra." I was contemplating whether to say or not. When he was leaving from the main door, I said thank you genuinely for the first time. He smiled towards me as he understands how I am feeling.

"No need Sir I know what you are feeling. If I was in your position I may do the same so no need to thank Sir. It is my duty." He was a young doctor aged around 28. I was feeling bad about threatening him but in that situation I can't control my emotions.

Then I closed the door and locked it. I went to my bedroom and called Sameer to inform about the situation. I walked to the balcony and spoke to him about Nikki's accident. I don't want to disturb her as she is sleeping soundly.

"You can come tomorrow and meet her. You have not met her since marriage. As you are my only family I want you to meet Nikki." He said he will come tomorrow and hung up. I came from the balcony door after speaking to Sameer, I saw that she woke up. I came hurriedly towards her to check if she was ok or not.

I scolded her for being careless but she did not hear any word I think so by looking at her face. She avoided looking at me. I was worried about her but she did not seem to care much. When she asked me to take to the bathroom I wanted to laugh at her looking at her face. She was really feeling awkward asking for my help. But when I am here, she feels embarrassed to ask her husband. I carried her to the washroom but I felt like kissing her now then and there looking at her beautiful face. I was remembering last night's events, when I felt her lips on my lips. It was a beautiful moment for me as it was my first kiss.

When I felt her staring at me I turned my front and carried towards the bed touching her body. I arranged the pillows to make her comfortable and went to prepare dinner. I prepared upma as it is easy and fast. I know basic cooking. I called the cook and maid to inform them to come tomorrow. I served it on the plates and took it to the room.

When I entered she was looking outside through the balcony door where the moon is shining giving the whole glow to the room. I was mesmerized looking at her features. Her eyes speak a thousand words.

"Uh..uh." I cleared my throat to gain her attention. She turned towards me hearing the sound. She tried to get up but I came fast towards her and helped her in sitting position keeping a pillow behind her back for support.

"Can you cook? I did not even know that you can cook food. I thought you do even enter into the kitchen. Now what did you prepare? Upma?" She thought I cannot cook but she doesn't even know what talents I have. I smirked looking in her direction feeling proud of myself and smiled to myself. I sat in front of her and kept both plates in between us.

"Open your mouth." Her mouth tightly shut when I kept the spoon in front of her to feed her. She was shocked, I can see it clearly on her face. Her widened eyes made me realize what she was feeling.

Slowly she opened her mouth. I fed her with the spoon. I can see tears forming in her eyes. A tear escaped from her right eye. She did not stop them then another tear left.

"Other than my papa, nobody fed me like this. Thank you for taking care of me. Another thing I want to say. Don't say anything to my papa about the accident. He will get tense. I will say to him when the time comes but not now. Is it Ok?" She said to me crying and asked to not say anything about her condition. I was contemplating whether to accept her condition or not. As it will be not fair to say about his daughter's condition later. But I think she has a point. He is a blood pressure patient so she can decide whether she wants to say it or not.

"It is very good. It is surprising to me that you can cook. You also eat na. It will get cold. If it is cold it does not taste good." I fed her the whole plate of upma and rubbed her mouth with water. When I touched her lips with my fingers, I felt an electric sensation throughout my body. I shivered slightly at the touch but I did not show it on my face what I felt at that moment. I gave her the tablets and water to drink. With a stinky face she gulped the tablets when I gave her a threatening look.

Then I helped her to lay down and covered her body with a duvet. She slept fast as the medicines worked. I slept on the other side of the bed looking at her and touching her with my both hands. I can't resist my hands whenever I am near her.

I kept my one hand on her stomach to not hurt her and slept peacefully after a long time. I woke up due to the moaning voice, when I saw that she was groaning in pain and holding her forehead with one hand, I was worried.

"It is hurting. Ayush. It is painful." When she saw me I woke up. She held my hand tightly which was on her stomach and was crying continuously.

"It's ok. It will go away. Wait for sometime. The doctor said it will be painful for a few hours. Please bear with it. I am there with you." I hugged her sideways, keeping my one hand under her head, another stroking her hair lightly. She was crying, keeping her head on my chest, sobbing continuously, unable to bear the pain. I don't even know when she slept but when I heard her snoring after a few minutes. I felt relief and continued stroking her hair and did not remove my body from her. I slept after kissing on top of her head, holding her tightly in my arms.

Authors Note

Sorry for late update guys. I was busy. I will try to update fast. Thank you for voting who all voted for me. If you like my story please motivate me by voting and commenting. Thank you once again.

I Like You

Nikshitra's Pov:

I felt so much pain throughout my body because of the injuries last night. I cried so much because of the pain so he woke up from his sleep and said sweet words to me. I felt grateful for that. He was there with me when I needed him. He took care of me very well and I felt content. Thinking about yesterday night, I was happy that I fell from the stairs. He fed me with his hands. He cooked for me yesterday. I think I am in a dream because I can't imagine him doing anything for me.

I am grinning seeing his face who is in deep sleep. I woke up early in the morning so I am staring at my husband without any care in the world. He is looking so cute and handsome. His hair is touching his eyes which are disturbing him as he is frowning in his sleep. I slowly touched his hair with my fingers and moved them backwards, he smiled in his sleep. Slowly rubbing his scalp with my fingers, another hand touching his bearded cheek, I felt soft touching his hair. I smiled looking at his face. I want to kiss him now looking at his handsome features, sharp jaw, cute nose, pouty lips, mesmerizing eyes and thick eyebrows.

I slowly leaned forward taking care of my hand to kiss him on his cheek. I was afraid that he would get up, but looking at his deep sleep I made the bold step to move forward. My heart is racing fast when there is an inch gap between my lips and his cheek. I placed my lips on his left cheek moving closer to him, grabbing his shoulder for support. His skin felt so warm on my cold lips. I pecked once and was about to leave his cheek. He grabbed my hands and turned me back on the bed.

"Haaaa.... Leave me. What are you doing?" I was shocked. Shock would be an understatement as I never thought he would wake up from his sleep. My eyes and mouth opened wide looking at him. He was staring down at me with different kinds of emotions which I think is lust. He was sitting on top of me without putting weight on me in a kneeling position on my waist and holding my hands upwards at both sides of my head. I tried to get my hands out of his hold but he gripped it more tightly whenever I tried.

"What were you doing, Nikshu? I think I needed answers first. I thought you were shy at these things but no, you surprise me. And why did you kiss me? Are you taking advantage of me?" He smiled mischievously looking at me. I can't even speak a word as I dont what to answer him. He smirked looking at my face. He made a shocking face at the last sentence like if I am going to rape him. It is my fault that I kissed him. What will I tell him? Ok I will say that something was there on his cheek. Will he believe me? No, I don't think so.

"Nothing, some...thing wa...s there on yo...ur cheek so I tried to remove it. That's it", I stammered and got scared looking at his face who was ready to devour me. I think he got my lie looking at his face. He was bending forward towards my face. We were face to face with an inch gap between our noses, I closed my eyes afraid of what he was gonna do?

"I like when you get shy and do these things and say I did not do anything. You get anxious and stammer telling lies but your eyes and face can explain your truth. Don't lie to me because I can read your face very clearly. Is that clear?" I nodded and opened my eyes slowly looking at his. Then he placed his soft and smooth lips on my right cheek pecking it twice. Gathering his weight on top of my body, intertwining our both hands he stared deeply into my eyes as if asking permission to kiss my lips or not.

"Shit.", When he was close to my lips his mobile rang disturbing our moment. He does not want to leave me as I can read his face.

"Pick up. It may be urgent." I pleaded to him and tried to wriggle my hands from his hold. He got irritated by seeing my face and left the bed picking his mobile from the bed stand to the balcony. I was shocked by his behaviour and touched my cheek where he kissed me. I was feeling shy and a smile appeared on my face thinking about our moment. I cannot move my leg, slowly with the help of both my hands I dragged my body to a sitting position and kept my left leg on the ground. When I was moving my right leg with my hand which has plaster, he came towards me angrily and kept his hand on my shoulder abruptly stopping my movements.

"What are you doing right now? How many times should I say not to move? If you want anything you can call me for help. I will help you and today I am not going to the office. I will do my work from home only. Today Sameer is coming to our house as he wants to meet you. Is it ok for you? I didn't even ask your permission, I am sorry for that. He only called me to inform me that he is coming in the afternoon as he knows about your accident." He helped me to stand up, keeping his one hand on my waist and another held my hand. I felt warm as he touched me.

"Please walk slowly." He was moving fast holding me so I requested him to go slow. We slowly walked to the bathroom and till then he waited outside the door. I brushed and did my business. Again he helped me to lay on the bed.

"I will prepare breakfast and I will call the maid if she is coming or not? If you need anything, call me. This is your mobile as it is broken. I bought it yesterday but I forgot about it. Here it is. If you do not like it I will bring another one." He answered and went to the closet to bring something. I know that it was mobile when he answered. I was very happy when he bought his very first gift. I was grinning and sat hurriedly and took the mobile from him hurriedly without waiting for him to give it to me. I opened it and it is an Iphone 11 new edition. I gasped looking at that. No, I can't accept this as it is very expensive.

"No, I can't accept this. It costs very much. You can give me a small mobile which costs less. I can accept that." I said to him as I was feeling low to not accept his gift. I gave the mobile to him in his hand. I was happy a moment ago so he came and sat beside me.

"Think of it as your first gift from your husband. You have every right to accept. You are my wife now. So please accept it." He requested me to take the mobile and kept it in my lap and held my hands with his both hands. I took it seeing his pleading eyes. He smiled when I accepted it.

"You can use it now and if you get bored you can use it anytime. I have fed my number in your mobile. Check it and install all the apps you want. All passwords have been set so you won't have any problem." He went out after saying everything that was needed to know about the mobile.

He brought breakfast after sometime and he looks freshen up. I think he freshened up in another room. The breakfast is simple that is toast and butter. We both ate in the bedroom only. After cleaning up he went out saying he had some work to do.

"If you want anything, call Meena aunty. She will help you. I will be studying until then. I will tell Meena aunty to clean you up. She will be here in 5 minutes." He said and within 5 minutes Meena aunty came, helped me to clean my body with a sponge and changed my clothes. Meena Aunty is an old aged woman about 55yrs. I was feeling shy while she was helping me with small tasks.

"Maam, If you need anything I am downstairs. Let me know ma'am. I will prepare lunch till then." She warmly smiled at me speaking politely. I can feel motherly feelings through her talk. She is a nice lady.

"Thank you Aunty and please don't call me ma'am. You can call me Nikki." I said to her smiling when she was leaving.

"Ok Nikki. Take care beta." She left from there and I laid on the bed thinking about Ayush. I don't know when I slept. I woke up from the sound of someone laughing. It is like music to my ears. I rubbed my eyes with my hand and saw where the sound was coming from. That time only Ayush opened the door laughing while coming with his friend Sameer. I saw him on our marriage day.

"Hello Nikshitra. How are you doing?" He looked very cheerful and came to my side and sat on the stool which is on bedside.

"I am good Sameer. How are you?" I asked him to slowly get up in a sitting position removing the blanket from my body.

"I am fine. Is he taking care of you or not? Tell me. I will beat him. If he neglects or avoids you I will be there with you Nikki. I will support you as he does not care about me. He behaves arrogant with everyone. I am his friend but he does not treat me like I am his friend. So now you will be friends and now I will ignore him. It's a deal. I don't know you from now on. Who are you mister?" I laughed very hard when he questioned Ayush like that. He was shocked when he suddenly said he was not his friend from now onwards. Ayush glared at his friend's suggestion. He is very jovial and speaks whatever comes to his mind. My dear husband is glaring at both of us. He speaks nonstop. I can see it.

"Thank you Sameer. I laughed this much after a very long time. Ok it's a deal. We are partners from now on to irritate Ayush." I whispered the last sentence slowly near Sameer's ear.

We talked about my college life and about my dad. We three ate lunch in the bedroom only. Ayush is glaring at me whenever I speak to Sameer jovially. He is mumbling something to himself which I cannot hear.

"What?" I asked Ayush but he said nothing and sat quietly without speaking to us. Me and Sameer talked for a long time about our favourite Korean dramas. I never thought boys would also watch kdramas. But he is the total opposite. He also liked bts music like me. We were laughing hard talking about the funny scenes in our shows. We have a lot in common so we easily clicked. I think I got a best friend because of my husband.

In the evening he left after drinking some tea. He said he will come to meet me every weekend. I was happy when he said that. Ayush was looking sad when I became sad while Sameer was leaving. He promised that Sameer will come every weekend.

I got excited and hugged him tightly when he cared about my happiness as he gave me a promise. I was on the bed and he sat beside me taking my hand giving a promise.

"Ilikeyouverymuchayush." I smiled hugging keeping my both hands on his shoulders behind his neck. I realized what I told him. I gasped surprised and was about to leave him but he hold me tight in his arms.

"What did you say?" He asked me but I kept mum. I know he heard it clearly so I hid my face in his shoulder smiling to myself.

---Authors note

Sorry for late update guys. I am busy these two weeks. I will try to update minimum 2 chapters per week. Please bear with me. It is my first time writing so I take so much time to write each chapter. I have to check it twice if there are any mistakes or not. Please vote and comment if you like this chapter. Thank you very much for giving me a chance to write and for all who have motivated me.

His Mom

Authors Note:

First of all thank you readers who all voted for my story. I am not a social person but I will try to interact with you guys as much as possible. I did not expect that my story would get these many views. It is very surprising for me as it is my first time writing. Please bear with me if I made any grammatical mistakes. If you have any doubts, message or comment me.

Ayush Pov:

I am grinning like a fool seeing her face hidden in my shoulder. She said I like you to me. She may think I did not understand when she spoke fastly but I understood clearly. I am very happy as she finally confessed to me.

"Nothing," she said, hiding her face in my chest. I gently moved her face with my hand from my chest and came face to face with her. We were staring at each other without blinking. At that moment I felt like kissing her but I controlled myself as I have been doing this lately so much.

"I think you said something like 'I like you'. Then why are you hiding yourself after confessing to me. I know it is your first time confessing , so don't worry I will not tease you. It is my first time." I said to her indirectly. I know very well she is shy after saying her feelings to me. She is blushing profusely as I can see her red cheeks. After saying the last sentence she grinned looking at me. After a second she realized what I said and got confused and asked the question which was roaming in her mind.

"What do you mean? Do you also have the same feelings for me? Please tell me na." She made a puppy face looking at me as if I was going to answer her question. I smirked looking at her reaction, so I thought to tease her more.

"I said it is also my first time kissing. I never kissed any girl before you. You are lucky you know that I am your first kiss who has never touched any girl." She was looking at me with a tearful expression and hugged me tightly, keeping her hands around my neck.

"I know as You don't know how to kiss the same as me." She was crying while talking to me and I got emotional when she was opening up to me about her feelings. I was doing wrong but I can't forgive her yet.

"I also like you Nikshitra. It is my first time saying this to any girl. I was afraid in my childhood that if I like any girl and if she rejects me after proposing. I can't bear it so I never used to speak to girls. My mom used to say when I meet my understanding partner you can share everything with her without feeling what they might feel of your actions. My mom used to say that if you can accept her in your life without changing yourself then you should remain with her throughout your life as I can't get a better life partner than her. So I am ready to be with you throughout my life Nikki." I said true words which were said by my mother. She was the only one who was the reason for my good upbringing. She used to say girls are very delicate as they will get broken easily when they have heartbreak. I was crying while saying my feelings to Nikki as I don't know if she will be there in my life or not. But I want to express my feelings for real.

But then I remembered that she is the reason for my misery and changed my expression thinking about her sins. I was very angry now but I smirked thinking how she easily melted to my words. I have to be very careful about my heart as I can't be pitiful towards her. It is an act to trust me without any doubt.

"Nikki, I will always protect you and take care of you. I will also take care of your dad. You don't have to worry, just trust me Nikki. I was not in my mind when I shouted at you on our marriage day. I was in tension at that time. Someone told me that you are bad and characterless. So I trusted his words and scolded you with bad names and slapped you. I am really sorry Nikki. I should have trusted you at that time. I got to know that the rumour which has been spread about you was false from my investigator. I was afraid that you would leave me so I changed my behaviour after knowing the truth. I liked you for a very long time so I requested your dad for your hand in marriage as I don't believe in love and all. Once again I am really sorry Nikki. Please forgive me. Trust me I won't believe anyone says bad things about you. I will believe in you only. " I am on cloud nine as my plan is working perfectly. I was afraid that she may not trust me as I have slapped her and scolded her with bad names, so I made up a story to believe in me.

I don't know that she already started trusting me after taking her to her dad's house . She has to trust me and love me then I can break her mentally and physically. It is the beginning of her end. All may think I am taking advantage of her situation but whatever she did to my family it is very less pain she is suffering. But.sometimes I feel pain when she is in pain or crying, I have to ignore it,

Revenge is my priority as of now. I like whenever she is close to me or kisses me. I got angry when she spoke to Sameer as he was her long lost friend. She was laughing with him like she never laughed in her whole life. She speaks non stop with him, what is there in him that I don't have. Why can't she speak to me Like that?

I know I am a boring and moody person but she can talk to me and I will listen to her. For a minute I thought I was jealous of Sameer but I don't think so. I am thinking too much about her, that's why my mind is playing games with me.

She broke the hug and started ignoring me as she turned her face away, not looking at me. She was feeling awkward after confessing her feelings first I know as I can see her nervous state. So I left her there without embarrassing her more. I can't act more in front of her. So to avoid that situation I left from there in anger to my study. I had to distract myself so I worked more. I slept in my study only not realizing how my eyes closed automatically due to tiredness.

After one week:

Nikshitra's Pov:

My life changed after confessing my feelings to Ayush. He is taking care of me daily. He did not even let me do single work. He completely changed, he helps me with everything I need without even telling him. He feeds me daily. He shifted my belongings to his room and I sleep daily in his room only as he gave me the orders to not put my leg outside of this room till I completely heal.

He took leave from his office for three days. In those three days I felt like a queen. He carried me everywhere I wanted without any complaint. He behaved very nicely with me. He always smiles at me. He used to bring snacks for me from outside. I used to eat lots of junk food whenever I was at home. I told him about that once then he brought it the next day. I was very happy that time when he brought chocolate ice cream with junk food. I ate all of that this week without leaving Ayush.

Whenever Ayush was not there, Meena aunty took care of my needs. She was there with me and changed my clothes daily and used to give me a sponge bath as my wounds are not completely healed.

Doctor came and checked today and he said it may take another week to completely heal my leg. So he said to be careful and not to move anywhere.

"Nikki, what are you thinking?" Ayush asked the question, came beside me and sat on the other side of the bed holding my right hand in his both hands. He is looking at me to give the answer to his question.

"Nothing, I was thinking about my life. How it changed drastically. I never thought I would marry a person who can have the same feelings as me. I did not think that he would reciprocate. Forget about that ,why are you late? Is there any problem in the office?" I was worried when he came late from the office. As usual he used to come in between 6:30 to 7pm. But today he came an hour late. I was ready to call him just now. He was smiling seeing my tense face.

"Don't worry sweetheart, there is a minor problem in the office. Someone in my office has betrayed and given the quotations to the other company. So the tender has gone to them. I don't know who did that. So we are searching but we have not got any positive result. Let's forget about this. I want to have a peaceful sleep with you." He said about the problem in his office. I want to change his mood so I diverted his mind by requesting him.

"I don't want to sleep Ayush. From morning till evening I am lying on this bed. Other than my mobile I don't have any work to do. Since this morning I have been scrolling through my instagram and watching kdramas. It is getting boring. Please take me to the living room. I have been seeing these four walls only from one week. I want fresh air. Pleaseeeeee.....Ayush." I made a cute pout face requesting him to take me from here. I can understand him as he was very tired from work so to change his mood, I made a request as I cant move from one place to another. It is getting congested to live in one room for a whole week.

So he carried me bridal style in his arms, without changing his clothes and took me to the garden. I wound my arms around his neck and stared at him continuously without blinking. I was smiling heartily when we reached the garden.

"Thank you Ayush." He settled me on the grass and sat beside me holding my shoulder.

"Its Ok. You will be fine within a week and you can do your normal routine. I know it is very tiring to sit in one room. I forgot that you need fresh air. You must be feeling congested sitting there alone. I am sorry." I regretted asking him to take me here. He was feeling bad because of me. He was tired and I am complaining. I should have thought about this. I am feeling bad. But I will remove his worries.

"Ayush please don't say sorry for everything which is not in our hands. I should say sorry to you as I did not even let you sleep. You were tired coming from office, I made a silly demand and without any complaint you accepted it." I said what I felt to him.

"Dont say like that Nikshu. Whatever you ask I will fulfill it. Now onwards no sorry. Ok." He said to me very sincerely, looking in my eyes while holding my hand in his hand. What I did to get this man. I got tears in my eyes feeling grateful to him.

I turned to the other side and wiped my tears without getting noticed. We were looking at the sky for half an hour without speaking a word, breathing fresh air. No words were spoken.

"In my childhood I used to watch stars with my mom. She used to say she wanted to go towards the sky and touch them. She was very fond of stars, whenever they twinkled she used to smile looking at them. I used to look at mom when she was looking at the stars. Now she has become the star leaving me alone in this world." One tear flowed from his left eye when he spoke about his mom. I was feeling pain in my heart when he shed a tear. I became sad thinking about his lonely life. I have my father with me but he dont have anyone to share his worries with. I hugged him to my chest and let him cry. He was reminiscing his memories of his mom. It will be painful for him. I also got tears in my eyes looking at him. I patted his back to let him go off his pain.

---Authors note:

Thank you readers for supporting me. If you like this chapter please vote and comment.

Taking Out

Authors Note:

Sorry guys for late update. I am busy this week. I will try to update two times a week. Please bear with me. And sorry for any grammatical mistakes.

Nikshitra's Pov:

Today I want to go out but how do I ask him? I am feeling suffocated being in this house. I have not gone outside since my marriage. I have recovered now. My wounds have healed. Ayush is taking care of me nicely. He does whatever I ask him.

This week he carried me and fed me. He took care of me like a baby. Whenever I smile I notice a spark in his eyes. Nowadays I talk to him freely without being afraid. He totally changed and I started to trust him more.

"Ayush, Are you free today?" I asked him nervously, biting my lip. I don't know what he will say. But I want to go outside of this house. As I asked he glanced up from his laptop while he was working sitting on his bed. He stared at me, questioning what I wanted.

"Why? What do you want?" He questioned blankly shifting his gaze to the laptop as it was the most important thing in the world. I got angry seeing his neglecting behaviour. I glared at him, keeping both hands on my hips.

"Ayuuushhhhh, Listen to me while I am speaking." I shouted at him and he swiftly turned towards me listening to my shouting. He glared back at me but I paid no attention to it. I don't fear him now. What will he do? He can do nothing if I threaten him that I will sleep in another room. Day before yesterday I threatened him and he obeyed me easily without any arguments as he couldn't sleep without cuddling me.

"What do you want, Nikshu? I am busy now. I have so much work pending. Speak fast. I don't have all the time for you. I am not free like you." I was hurt while he spoke like that. I was not important to him. I know he dont have all the time for me. I understand but how can he speak harshly to me? He spoke like I am a burden to him. My tears started to fall as I was deeply hurt. He got up from the bed and strode fast towards me seeing my tears.

"I am sorry Nikshu. I am sorry. Please forgive me." He hugged me tightly without letting me go as I wriggled in his hold while he apologised to me. I got out of his hold by pushing him with my hands on his chest.

"I am sorry that I disturbed you. I know that you don't have all the time for me. I can understand that you are tired from office work. I know I am not important to you. You can have your time with your laptop. Once again I am sorry for disturbing you while you were doing your important work." I wiped my tears from my eyes and walked away from our room. I know I should not have spoken like that but I am angry that he is not spending time with me. I stomped my feet after entering the kitchen. I will cook my food and watch some series.

I decided I will not talk to him. I can also work. But I don't want to work as of now. I want to spend time with myself. I want to take a break. I can work in any office with my qualifications. I will start to apply for a job tomorrow. What does he think of me? That I am a freeloader. No, I will prove to him that I can also work.

"Nikshu...Please I am sorry na.. please forgive me." He back hugged me keeping his hands on my bare waist and face on my shoulder. With his one hand he is drawing circles with his fingers on my bare waist. I was ticklish so I started to wriggle but he held me tightly with his other hand. I moved away as I couldn't control my giggle. I have to be angry I thought but he knows that I am ticklish whenever he touches my sides. So he slowly started tickling on one side of waist. As I was wearing silk saree I can feel his fingers on my body. I giggled continuously while he tickled my sides without stopping. He laughed with me while I was leaning backwards towards him holding his both hands to stop this torture. But he did not stopped till I laughed heartily with him.

When I was out of breath he stopped tickling and turned my body facing towards him staring continuously smiling at me.

"Please don't be angry. I will do whatever you want. I swear. You are very important to me. I was busy at that time and you came when I was angry. So I spoke nonsense to you." He pinched his neck with his thumb finger and forefinger. He was looking so cute and I forgave him as he apologised 3 times.

"Ok I forgive you. I want to go out with you today. I am feeling suffocated living in these four walls. So I want to ask you, can we go out?" I smiled, keeping my both hands on his shoulders and his hands on my waist. Our bodies were close and there was no gap between us.

"Ok, Where do you want to go?" He asked me then I grinned. He was suspicious looking at my smile. I grabbed his hand and went to our room with him.

"Change your clothes. I will wait for you in the living room." I ordered him, he was looking surprised but he obeyed me. He came after five minutes wearing blue jeans and white shirt looking hot and handsome. My mouth hung open while he was descending like a model rolling his sleeves. He came face to face with me and raised his eyebrows asking me 'what'. I shake my head as if nothing.

He intertwined our hands and grabbed the car keys but I took the keys from his hand.

"What are you doing? Give the keys to me." He glared at me while I hid the keys in my hand and held it backwards.

"Today we will not go in the car. We will use public transport." I said staring directly with an unwavering gaze. He was angry. I can see that. But I will not listen to him today.

"What? Are you mad? Give me the keys first. We cannot go on public transport. What will people think about me? And the media will not leave me if they see me in public transport with you." He said to me glaring back. But I will not back down.

"You said you will do whatever I want. So I want to go by bus. You will come with me. No one will notice you if you wear a cap. You are not a celebrity as you are feeling." I said casually and lightly and he opened his mouth wide listening to me. It doesn't matter to me. I want to enjoy myself freely today.

"Ok give me one minute. You won't listen to me. What I am doing because of your craziness. If I am in news tomorrow, I will not spare you." He threatened me but I did not care. He ascended the stairs leaving me alone in the living room. He came wearing a cap and goggles looking like a hot model leaving his top buttons open. I want to kiss him then and there. I want to see his naked chest.

"Close your mouth and come fast." I followed him after waking up from my dreamland. He was walking fast towards the main gate. I can't match his steps.

"Ayush. Wait." I called from back running towards him. He turned back, keeping his both hands in his pockets watching me running.

"Ok now there will be no bus from here directly. What do you want to do now?" He questioned me and I was out of breath while running. I held my one hand towards him and caught my breath first.

"We wi.. will go in auto from here to the bus stop. Then we will board the bus." I said to him like I am an intelligent one here.

We booked an auto from uber. I was feeling fresh air watching the trees surrounding us. He sat beside me without even uttering a word. So I turned towards him to talk to him.

"Ayush. Are you uncomfortable?" I asked nervously as I don't know what he is feeling.

"No.. I am good Nikki. I am comfortable. No need to worry about me. You enjoy it." He spoke smiling to me holding my one hand with his.

After some time we got down in front of the bus stand. It was not crowded as it is the weekend today. He paid for the auto and was standing in the bus stop. We were waiting for the bus. After five minutes one bus came. I want to go anywhere where the bus takes me. We boarded the bus.

All were looking at him as he came from a different planet. He was looking uncomfortable. We took our seats and I sat near the window. Most seats were empty as it is sunday. Only a few people were there in the bus. He sat beside me and held my hand tightly as if he was scared.

"What happened? If you want we will get down now." I said to him as I could see he was more uncomfortable. His face looks like he is scared. So I held his hand between my both hands and kept in my lap.

"No..No..Nothing. When I was in school. We used to go daily in the bus only. We were poor when we were small. I know how I felt when I used to travel in bus. It was good going with friends and walking with them to school and coming to house." He told about his past and I genuinely smiled listening to him. But I want to ask why he is telling 'We'. As I know he doesn't have any siblings. I think he is talking about Sameer.

"I have travelled by bus my whole life. We can't afford a school bus so I used to travel by bus while going to school and college. My dad used to go to the office so I got into the habit of travelling in public transport. I used to enjoy it with my friends. We used to eat panipuri while coming home." I told how I also used to travel by bus. He was listening to me attentively. Some people were glancing curiously as he was wearing a cap. Some girls were taking photos of him as they recognised him. But he didn't care about that as he noticed. He was only looking at me, smiling towards me. I turned to the other side as blush was forming on my cheeks. As I looked outside the window I saw a multiplex.

"Movie." I shouted and held his hand then we both got down there after paying the fare. He looked shocked at first but he regained his posture and came with me. Ayush wore his goggles as some girls were ogling him. He held my hand and we both walked towards the ticket booth.

"Which movie do you want to watch?" He asked me and I checked all the movies which were available.

"Lovestory." I said to him and he took the tickets standing in the queue. I was mesmerised that he is doing all these things for me.

He came and we both went to the cinema hall taking popcorn and coke with us. We both sat in our respective seats. He booked the corner seats. I was grinning and was feeling very happy. It is my first movie with Ayush.

"Are you comfortable?" He asked me politely and I was smiling to myself how he was caring about me so much.

"I am fine. Are you ok?" I asked him and he nodded. Through half way of film we were holding our hands together. Afterwards he kept his one hand on my shoulder and put my head on his shoulder. I leaned towards him. It was my wish to watch a movie with my husband hugging him. It came true. We ate popcorn and saw the film asking a few questions in the middle about the film. We came out after the film ended. It was a good film. We enjoyed it very much.

"I am hungry. I want to eat chinese." I demanded Ayush and he pouted looking at me.

"Come I will take you to a good resta..." He said but I interrupted him.

"No, we will eat street food not in some hifi restaurant. All will recognise you there. I want to eat noodles on the street." I pouted and made a cute face asking him.

He obeyed me silently without arguing as he knows I will win the argument. We took an auto from there to a Chinese stall.

I ordered spicy noodles and manchurian. I devoured like an hungry animal. He was watching me amazingly as he did not watch any girl eat like that. He also ate noodles but it was very spicy so he wasn't able to handle the spiciness, water started flowing from his eyes. He drank two glasses of water and opened his mouth gasping for air. I felt sorry for him and bought a dairy milk from a nearby shop and gave it to him. He ate it fast.

After some time he became normal and ordered less spicy fried rice for him. We ate ice cream while returning to our house. I took two double chocolate cornettos and he took butterscotch ice cream. I was licking my ice cream without caring about anyone. He was watching me continuously while I was eating my ice cream.

"What?" I asked him but he replied nothing. I was in my world of ice cream without caring and walking on the road. He was walking beside me staring and eating his ice cream from time to time.

"You live to eat. I understood one thing about you is you don't care about anyone while you and your food is in front of you. You will forget the world when your favourite food is in front of you. I don't know where the food goes in your body as you are always slim." He spoke smiling and I glared at him as he said I am a foodie. But it is a fact that I love food. I don't diet how much I eat. How much I eat I cant get fat as my body type is slim.

We went home in the auto as it was evening. We enjoyed it a lot and I am feeling happy after so many days.

"I am very tired." As we entered the house I sat on the sofa leaning my head on the head rest closing my eyes.

"Sleep now. I have some work . I will complete it in the study and don't disturb me till then. Ok?" He said and went away.

"Ok Sir." I saluted him and lied down on the sofa closing my eyes feeling tired.

--Authors Note:

Thank you for 2.5k views. Thank you who all voted and commented my story. If you like this chapter please vote and comment. If any mistakes are there then I am sorry. I will try to correct if you comment where I have to change. Thank you once again

Periods

Authors Note

Sorry for the late update guys. I was busy with my personal issues. I will update whenever I am free. Please bear with me. Thank you for 8k views. I never thought that I will get these many views. I deeply apologize for my late update. Please bear with my grammatical mistakes. Please follow me guys if you like my story. Please vote if you like this chapter. I will update according to your votes guys.If it is 25 votes for this chapter. I will update next chapter fast. Thank you guys for supporting me--Ayush Pov:

I am smiling to myself thinking about today's events. I cannot concentrate on my work as my thoughts are always about her mischievous side who doesn't care about what she is doing. She never asks for money nor does she spend a lot. She likes small things which make her happy like food. She is emotional and acts like strong but I can see through her. She is average looking girl but beautiful from heart. I like that about her. She is quiet sometimes thinking about me or her dad. She doesn't care about anyone else when the most important people are around her. I realized that she does not trust anyone easily to open up about herself. It takes time for her to realize whether it is good or bad. I left my work and decided to sleep in our room.

It is strange that in one month she changed me.

When I entered our bedroom, the lights were off. So I turned on the lights to see the bed was empty. Where is she? I thought she was tired, so she fell asleep. But she is nowhere to be seen.

"Nikki...Nikki... where are you?" I am shouting running downstairs as I was getting worried. It was midnight and there was no response from her. I felt something happened to her like last time. But the scene in front of me made me open my mouth widely. When I was at the last step I noticed that she was sleeping on the sofa. She is snoring, lightly opening her mouth a little. Saree has been misplaced due to her continuous shifting in that small sofa. I can see her cleavage, waist and half part of her legs. I closed my mouth coming out of my dreamland and went towards my prey who was slightly frowning in her sleep.

I took small steps towards her and sat down on the floor mesmerizing her beauty in front of me. I slowly touched her face with my fingers. I started to remove her hair strands which were disturbing her sleep and tucked under her ear. I gently touched her forehead to remove her frown. She slightly pouted like inviting me to kiss her. I can't control myself if she behaves like this. My eyes are devouring her body just by looking at her flawless skin. I want to kiss every inch of her body without leaving any part. My fingers are itching to touch her unknown places. I moved forward to peck her forehead by kneeling down on the floor. I placed my lips on her forehead, then moved forward to kiss her eyes. I kissed both eyes, not disturbing her sleep. I moved forward to kiss her round cheeks and then nose. Atlast I pecked her lips once, twice, thrice. She slightly stirred in her sleep and moved her face to the other side, So I climbed on the sofa placing my hands on either side of her breast, not placing my whole weight on her.

My sensuous gaze is ready to devour her completely but I know she is not ready. But I can't control myself seeing her half naked body. I placed lips on her jaw for sometime and moved to her throat where her adam's apple is moving up and down breathing heavily. With my hand on her chin. I moved towards her collar bone, not leaving any part without my kisses. I kissed her collar bone and moved upwards on the junction of neck and throat and bit there slightly with my teeth as my hands were roaming at the sides of her breast. When I bit she screamed loudly, making me frightened.

"Ahhhhh....Leave me you jerk." She woke up instantly being shocked, pushing me with her hands. I looked up to her face and stared at her without speaking a word. When she came face to face with me she took deep breaths opening her mouth slightly not speaking a word. I held her both hands in a tight grip which were placed on my chest. I placed my body weight on her and shifted her hands upwards with my hand holding it.

"Wh...aaat are youuu do...ing Ayuuuu..sh?" She stuttered, frightened of what was happening with her. I stared intensely not removing my gaze from her eyes which held fear.

"This.." I said and captured her lips with mine. I started slowly moving my lips on her upper lip, then I pecked her red luscious lips staring right through her eyes as if I wanted to claim her right now. I kissed her passionately, not leaving any part of her lips. Slowly I placed my lips on her lower lip leaving her breathless. Not giving a gap I started to bite her lower lip, my hands roaming around her body continuously, touching her sensually with my fingers.

"Fuckkkk.." I cursed when she unintentionally touched my throbbing dick with her knee. I closed my eyes feeling pain there. I slowly opened my eyes to see her gasp and within a second she started to laugh uncontrollably. I was shocked when she laughed seeing my situation. I never thought that she could laugh in this situation.

"I...I a..m so...sorry." she said between her laughs not caring about me. I was perplexed by her actions. How can she laugh at me??? She can change any romantic situation to comedy. I moved away from her glaring at her. But she did not stop her laughing session. But suddenly got up from the sofa and ran from there to our room, running fastly. I don't know what happened. So I decided to check and walked to my room.

She was not there as I was leaving the room. I heard sounds from the washroom. I knocked on the bathroom door. But she did not respond. Again I knocked twice.

"Are you okay Nikki? What happened?" I was getting nervous as she did not reply to me. After a few seconds of silence she opened the door and walked past me hiding from my face. She is not seeing me. She is staring downwards and nervously fidgeting her fingers not speaking a word.

I touched her shoulder with my one hand and with another I lifted her face placing my fingers on her chin. I can see tears gathered in her eyes ready to fall.

"Nikki.. What happened sweetheart? Are you hurt somewhere? Tell me. Please look into my eyes." I pleaded as I don't know what is bothering her. After looking at her face I realized what the problem was. She avoided looking into my eyes.

"Did you got your period?" After asking this she immediately lifted her eyes staring at me and opened her mouth in surprise as she did not expect to guess her problem.

"Do you want sanitary napkins? Don't feel embarrassed Nikki. It is every girl's problem. I will bring it to you. Don't worry. Do you need anything other than these?" I asked her if she needs any chocolate if she gets cramps. Tears flowed from her eyes and hugged me tightly, keeping both hands around my torso. She cried so much. I don't know what happened to her. I soothingly rubbed her back and placed my chin on her forehead.

"Thank you Ayush. I need chocolates and Green Lays as of now." I smiled thinking about her love for food. In this situation she also made me smile. I thought she would not ask me anything but she surprised me.

I gently removed my hold from her and removed all the traces of her tears from both cheeks and kissed her smooth skin lightly.

"Take care. I will bring the necessities, till then you freshen up." I left the room and drove to the supermarket which is 2 kilometers away from the house which is open 24 hours as it is midnight. I brought what all she needed. I don't know which brand she uses so I brought all packets of different sizes. I forgot to ask her as I realized that after going there.

The woman at the billing counter continuously stared at me as she was seeing an alien. When I was at the billing counter the woman asked me who I was buying these many.

"For my Wife ma'am. Thank you." I left the supermarket seeing their gasping faces as she never expected I am married. I think she recognized me from the tabloids. My mom taught me when I was in teens. She told me about the menses that all girls go through at a certain age. I never felt ashamed as my mom told me what all pain girls go through. From that time onwards whenever my mom was on her period I used to do all the work of the house except cooking. As I am least interested in cooking, I can do other household chores.

I bought 10 dairy milk chocolates and chips of so many varieties that she can eat all day long. She likes street food so I bought chinese noodles on the way which was open. After an hour I reached home and directly went to the bedroom to see her standing in the balcony gazing at the stars.

"Nikki. Here is what you need. If you need anything else. Tell me I will bring it for you." When she saw what all I brought in the plastic wrap.

"Are you serious? These many sanitary napkins?" Nikki gasped and shouted at me. Then realized her mistake and apologised. She smiled after gazing at me with care and emotions swirled in her both eyes. Tears gathered when she saw the food I bought for her.

"Thank you." She genuinely appreciated my effort with so much emotion on her face. I can feel what she is going through as she doesnt have her mother with her. She took the sanitary napkins and went to the bathroom.

After a few minutes she came and sat on the bed changing into a t-shirt and tracks. I laid down on my side of the bed and she slowly laid down and moved towards me facing me. Her both palms are pressed under her cheek gazing at me adorably like I am the most precious one. No words spoken between us.

"You know all my relatives used to say how can I survive without mother. They told my father to do a second marriage. But he never did as he feels he is betraying his love for his wife. My dad used to love my mom so much. After 5 years of their marriage my mom conceived me. Doctor said about the complications but my mom was stubborn to keep me. My dad told that she took promise from him about taking care of me. She said to him that I will be my dads life as there was no one for him. So many have bullied me as I dont have my mom. But I was very happy with my dad. As he took care of me throughout his life without caring about himself. I never felt missing my mom as dad was there for me. But at the age of thirteen I got to know about the need of mother. As I don't know about periods at that time, I got scared seeing blood. I thought I got hurt and said to my dad about the stomach ache I was feeling. He explained me like a mother explains to her daughter. I was crying so much that day and he also told what girls will go through till certain age. My dad was there with me through every pain I gone through. He brought the sanitary napkins and explained me how to wear it. He also bought chocolates as he said the pain will subside after eating it. That's why I am addicted to junk food, my dad used to bring me so much food as he cannot see his doll to cry in pain. I never told about the cramps I used to feel because he may get tensed. So I kept my strong facade in front of him as I could see worry in his eyes. He used to understand and told me to skip the school and college whenever I was on period." She smiled through the tears which are flowing freely from her eyes. She told about her life what she went through at the most important phase of her life. A tear escaped from my eye listening her talking about her dad. I gathered her in my arms and tightly hugged her placing her face in the crook of my neck.

I gently soothed her back with my fingers holding her in my embrace. Then sleep overtook us both.

The morning sunlight rays attacked me and I stirred slightly removed my hands from Nikki who was snuggling in my neck. I rubbed my eyes and shifted Nikki on the pillow, not disturbing her sleep.

I pecked her forehead shifting her hair tendrils from her face under her ear. I smiled watching her face and remembered last night talk. I know her life has been tough but I can't forget she is the reason for my life's destruction. My smile faded as I was committing a sin but I can't forget and forgive her. I went to freshen up and done my jogging.

"Hello, Who is this?" My mobile rang and I lifted the call as to who will call early in the morning. I thought it may be Sameer who calls for urgent office work. But it is an unknown number, I frowned when there was silence on the other side.

"Hello Sir, I am speaking from the XYZ news channel. Is it true that you are married Sir?" I groaned thinking about how they know about my marriage. So I cut the call without responding to him and checked today's news on my mobile.

All the news was about me roaming around the streets with Nikki. I was shocked but I know this will happen. I have to think of something to stop these rumours.

--Authors Note

Please follow me guys and vote this chapter if you like it. If maximum 25 votes for this chapter then I will update next chapter faster guys. Thank you once again

Confession

Ayush Pov:

I need to think of a solution to get out of this mess. I thought that I would never show Nikki in front of the world as my wife. But I think I should change my plan.

"Sameer. I want you to arrange a party after three days and make all the preparations. Call all of our business clients and partners. Make sure to inform the press also." I called Sameer and was informed to arrange the party.

"Hello to you too, my best friend.. Are you mad or what? Disturbing me early in the morning. If you want anything, please do not order me. Is that clear?" He spoke annoyed at me, irritating me. I was not in a position to scold him as I want this matter to be solved but this idiot cannot understand.

"Okay. Now listen carefully." He cut me off as I angrily spoke to him as he was testing my patience.

"And why are you arranging a party? Is any deal finalised? You did not even inform me?" He asked me and I was clenching my fingers not able to tolerate him as he is not letting me complete my sentence.

"If you let me complete then I will tell you Sameer." I gritted my teeth and talked about the rumours that are spreading like wildfire.

"Oh sorry sorry. And why did you not reveal your marriage to the outside world?" He asked but I did not like the way he asked.

"That is my personal life, Sameer. You don't need to ask me." I angrily told him and cut the call. After closing my eyes for a few minutes to calm my anger and unclenching my both fists, I turned to the bed where she was sleeping peacefully.

She is looking so beautiful in her sleep. Automatically my lips turned into a smile looking at her face. But I have to execute my plan fast before it's too late. I have to control my feelings as it will lead to heartbreak only. I turned back and left the room without glancing at her remembering her deeds. I need to avoid her till she recovers as I don't know what I will do with her.

Nikshitra Pov:

For three days I did not see him. Where is he? How is he? I don't know. But I know one thing that he is avoiding me intentionally. I thought he cared about me when he took care of me as I was on my period. I felt like a child when he was with me. But I think I am in a dream as he never enquired about me after that day. He did not even come home. He did not even inform me. I was tense the first day as he will come home regularly at night but he did not come. I was waiting the whole night for him as I tried calling him but it was switched off. Atlast he informed me through his secretary that day he will not be coming home. Next day I thought he would come home but he surprised me by not showing me his face.

Whenever I call him he is saying he is busy or he cuts the call. I cried today because of him as I feel alone in the house. I won't talk to him. What does he think of himself that he will do whatever he wants huh? As I was in my thoughts sitting on the sofa someone entered through the main door. As it is dark I cannot see but I guess it is Ayush. I know it is him. So I did not even take a glance at him. I was very angry at him so without sparing a glance at him I walked towards our room.

"Nikki. Listen to me." He followed me but I did not even look at him as I sat on the bed and lied down, turning backwards to him pulling the duvet over me.

"Please just once talk to me. I am sorry that I was busy with my work. I should have told you but my presence was important. I should have come home, I know but I did not think that you would be this much angry at me." He held my shoulder in one hand and was trying to turn me towards his side but I was removing his hand but he made a strong grip not allowing me to remove. Tears gathered in my eyes but I did not allow any of my tears. I want to let my anger out and shout at him. But I think I should give him the silent treatment as he knows the value of me who is waiting impatiently for him.

"Nikki..Nikki..Nikki.. I know you are thinking that I am avoiding you but Noo. I am not avoiding you. Really, I am sorry. Please forgive me. I did not apologise so many times to any person. It is you only. So talk to me." I was about to burst any moment but I remained calm counting numbers in my mind, keeping my eyes closed.

"So you realised that you have home huh? You were busy na go and live in that office only. Why did you come here and who am I to tell you. Oh sorry I forgot that you are THE GREAT AYUSH KHURANA. You can do whatever you want but you forgot that your wife is waiting for you. You know what I DON'T CARE.." I snapped at him as I can't control my anger anymore and pushed his hands from me. I was crying continuously and pushed his shoulders hitting him with my hands on his chest.

"I thought you cared about me but no you did not even call me once to check on me. What should I think huh? You were with your love that is your work and I am here waiting for you. I was worried that you had your food on time or not.I thought something happened to you when you did not answer your call. Did something happen to you? No.. you are well and good and I was not eating my food on time as I was freaking worried about you. Once you apologise you think I will forgive you. Noo. Never." I was literally shouting at him with continuous crying but he did not move his lips for once as he sat there paralyzed because of my actions.

"Why are you worried?" He asked me one question which made me silent as he was holding both of my hands from hitting him. I stared at him wide eyed as I realized that he became my everything. I silently stared at him with an open mouth as I thought of answering him as I like him. But I know it will be a lie as it is more than like.

"I...I.. don't know" I said to him and he looked like he knew what I was thinking.

"So you don't know? But why are you angry at me? You know, I goto office but never you did not behaved like this. What is wrong now?" He asked me, and came face to face without leaving an inch gap touching our noses. I was breathing heavily due to our close proximity, my heart is running a marathon.

"Wh..Why did you not come? I was worried thinking about you." I spoke gathering some courage staring in his eyes.

I flinched when he left me without bothering about me.

"You love him, idiot. You did not even realize that he became your world. Tell him fast before it's too late" My subconscious said to me.

I slapped my forehead for realizing this late. I have to tell him. But how should I tell him? Will he love me like I love him? If he rejects me also it is okay as I know no one can love somebody like me. But I have to confess my feelings whether he rejects me or not. I will take care of him and love him unconditionally if he loves me or not.

After sometime he came into the bedroom but did not even spare me a glance as I was staring at him continuously.

He lay down on his side turning his back to me.

" So you are doing the same to me. Okay. As you wish." I muttered and turned my back towards him lying on the bed.

I was disturbed by the sounds beside me. As he is continuously tapping the wood of the bedside lamp.

"What?" I muttered angrily, turning my face towards him. He is angry. I can see through his face. But I am more stubborn than you.

"Tomorrow there is a party. I want to announce to the world that you are my wife. I will send the makeup artists and designers for your outfit tomorrow. So dress accordingly and be ready by 7 at night." He said calmly clenching his jaw as if he is controlling his anger and turned the lights off without listening to my answer.

"No. I won't come with you. You can take anyone. But I won't come with you." I said to him as I thought he would fight with me but he did not even turn towards me. I was angry as he was not talking to me. I only have the right to be angry as he did the mistake. But I am suffering. I thought he would come for me and apologise. But I was wrong, his ego is bigger than him. I want to punch his face right now.

"Ayush..." I hit his shoulder with my right palm hard. He got up and looked angrily at me. I don't know why he is angry.

"What is your problem? You only said that I can take anyone with me. So I will take any girl with me as my wife. Okay. Are you happy? So now dont disturb me and let me sleep." He shouted at me and I flinched at his tone and my waterfalls started when he said he will take another girl as his wife.

"HOW DARE YOU? I am your wife. If you think of other women then I will kill you. Get that in your head." I shouted at him, grabbing his collar facing him. My eyes glaring at him. His hand sneaked through my waist slowly holding me in my place while I was in a kneeling position, the same as him glaring at each other.

"You only said that I can take anyone. So what is bothering you?" He asked me. I know he wants to know about my feelings towards him. But how should I express it? I can't even speak when he is holding me.

"That..That.." I stammered not knowing what to say and avoided his eyes looking down.

"What is that? Tell me Nikshu." He said softly holding my chin between his fingers.

"I..I..I. Love You Ayush." I finally confessed my feelings and hid my face in his chest smiling at myself.

"I love you too Nikki." He confessed and I was shocked. I moved my face from his chest and came face to face with him. He is staring at me with different emotions. He cupped my cheeks with both of his palms and came closer to me.

He looked in my eyes then at my lips asking for permission. I nodded. Without even giving me a second his lips came crashing onto mine.

---Authors Note

Thank you guys whoever read my story. I am really sorry for late update. Please vote and comment if you like this chapter. I am sorry if there are any grammatical mistakes. Please follow me if you like my story. Please vote guys if you like it.

Authors Note

Hello guys. I want your suggestion guys. To proceed further in my story. I want to know if you guys want mature content ahead in my next chapter or some romantic scenes? I will write mature content after some romance if you guys want? In next chapter I decided to write consummation but I want your suggestion guys. Because after consummation most chapters will be painful and less romantic. So if you want romance then I will postpone consummation. So please help me with your suggestion guys. Please write in comments what should I choose in next chapter.

Party

Authors note:

Thank you guys for supporting my story. If you like this chapter please vote and comment. I will try to update fast. Please ignore if any mistakes are there as I am new to this writing. Next chapter will be mature. Please follow me guys

Ayush Pov:

As I am kissing her I can feel her tears on my cheeks. Her pink lips were soft and moving in rhythm with my rough lips. I can feel her palms on my shoulders tightly clutching while I nibbled her soft lips. I slowly bite her bottom lip with my teeth moving my hands around her back not allowing her to breathe for a second. I am holding her securely in my arms both our bodies touching without any gap between us. After a few minutes she scratched my shoulder with her nails when I did not allow her to leave me. I hissed and left her lips in shock breathing heavily.

"Ah! It is painful. Why did you scratch me Nikki?" I asked her, rubbing the right side of my shoulder where she scratched. I can see that her nail marks were printed on my shoulder. I can see that four straight red marks are formed. I was unable to comprehend the situation as she started laughing.

"Ha...ha..You.. ha..are..acting..ha...liking a kid Ay..ush." I frowned seeing her face as she was enjoying my situation. I am acting like a kid? She is the one who is behaving like a kid scratching me. How dare she?

"Youuu. You only caused this. I am trying to be romantic here and I want to remember our special moment. But you have to destroy it. I was happy but you have to ruin my mood." I took the pillow and hit her head with it, taking my anger out. She stopped laughing when I had hit her and turned her face towards me pointing her finger as if she was angry but removed her finger and avoided looking at me after realizing what we were doing.

"Why di..d yo..u not le..t m..e breathe? I was trying to remove you..r hold but you didn't let me. So I did not got any option." She stuttered and shrugged her shoulders as if she wanted to avoid me. She did not meet my eyes as she realized the position of ourselves. So I pulled her to me in a hug.

"You don't have to feel embarrassed Nikki. I was just kidding with you. It is not our first kiss then why are you not looking at me. I will not do anything without your consent. Dont worry about that. Whenever you are ready, that time only we will move to the next step. Ok?" I asked her to keep calm and hugged her tightly to my chest. I know what she is feeling. She is thinking that I will consummate our marriage as we expressed our feelings. But I can't stoop to that level without her consent.

She is blushing now as I can see her red face hiding in my chest, her both hands at the back of my tshirt tightly clutching. I was caressing her hair with my one hand and another holding her side bare waist.

She nodded and was totally immersed in enjoying our moment, closing my eyes, resting my chin on her head smiling to myself.

"You are getting a call. Please lift it. It may be important, Ayush." She said to me and tried to push me with her hands but I didn't allow her to leave me as I don't want to take the call as I am feeling good in her arms forgetting my worries.

"This is the last time I am warning you. Leave me or I wil..l I will " I interrupted her looking into her eyes daring her what she will do?

"What will you do? Nothing. You can't leave me ever. Remember that. You belong to me." I was telling her staring into her eyes and she did the unexpected.

"Ahhhh." She pinched me in my stomach suddenly. I was shocked at first and rubbed the area where she pinched me.

"Why are you torturing me Nikki? What did I do to you? Are you taking your anger out on me for all of the times?" I made a pout and asked her, making a sad expression. She scrunched her nose glaring at me. She is looking too cute and I want to pinch her chubby cheeks but I will not do today as she is in an angry avatar.

"Hello Sameer. Why are you calling late at night?" I picked up the call as she was glaring and shifted her eyes to the mobile which was ringing continuously.

"Hello my dear friend. As you are not letting me sleep, how should I let you sleep. You have given me all the work to prepare for the party. I did not go home because of you and you are having your beauty sleep forgetting about your friend. How can you?" I know he is smiling and smirking at last acting as if he succeeded in his mission of disturbing my sleep.

"Have the decorations been completed and all the work has been done or not?" I asked him to ignore his nonsense talk controlling my anger for disturbing us.

"Yes, the work has been completed and you should come and check. If you want to change anything, tomorrow morning you can do it." He sensed my mood and answered normally.

"Ok tomorrow I will come to the venue. Thank you Sameer." I said before hanging up.

I did not realize when Nikki had slept lying on her side of the bed. I guess she is tired. Now it is early morning at 2 am. I was staring at her face then I realized what I was doing. She is making me feel different emotions but I have to mask it. First step of the plan succeeded. Now she trusts me. I know I did not love her. I like her but I know she is faking it. I know her real face.

I layed down thinking about my only family who brought happiness in my life after my parents death. Tears gathered in my eyes and one tear slipped from my right eye and rubbed my eyes thinking about the happy memories we have spent. I turned sidewards showing my back to Nikki. Seeing her face reminded me of my past. Switching off the lights I slept after some time turning and tossing after tiredness as I am now used to cuddling her. But today I did not feel like touching her or seeing her face. She is the reason why I am alone in this world. I will make sure to make her lonely in her whole life.

Next morning I woke up late and got ready to go to the venue wearing my navy blue suit with white shirt underneath and matching my outfit with red stripe tie. Nikki did not wake up as she slept late. I did not disturbed her sleep and wrote a note that I am going to the office and be ready till 7 pm.

I went directly to the venue and checked all the preparations. It is beautiful. I know I can trust Sameer in this. There is a nice swimming pool in the middle decorated with hanging lights around the area.

Next I called my PA to arrange the designers and makeup artists for Nikki. I know she doesn't know anything about makeup. For my reputation I have to present her accordingly as the press is also involved.

I went to the office after meeting the hotel manager.

Nikki Pov:

When I woke up I touched the other side of the bed to feel empty. Groaning and rubbing my eyes with both hands I checked the time on my mobile to get surprised as it is 12 o'clock in the afternoon.Then I remembered what happened last night I blushed remembering our confession. I never thought that he had the same feelings towards me. I was grinning from ear to ear remembering when we were about to do the deed last night. I know I am not ready.

Removing the blanket from me I got up and went to the bathroom to freshen up. I remembered Ayush told me about the party today at night.Then I saw the note which was placed on the dressing table and smiled seeing it.

"Nikki I am sending beauticians to our house. Be ready till 7pm. And dont be late for the party. I may get late so I will directly reach the venue. I will send the car to pick you up. So dont worry and eat your lunch as I know you may not get up until afternoon. So don't blame me for not eating your food on time. Yesterday you said because of me you are not eating your food. I think it is wrong of you to blame me. Whether I am there or not 'Eat your food on time Nikki'. Dont worry about me." I read thrice touching his letter with my both hands as it brought tears to my eyes. I was very happy that he cared about me and kept the note near to my chest smiling widely. I cooked lunch and ate it. I contemplated whether to call him or not. But I choose the other option to not call him as he may be busy with his meetings.

I am seeing the reels in my instagram of bts to time pass. I was lying down in my bed then I heard doorbell. I think makeup artists have came. I ran fast down the stairs and opened the main door to see two beautiful women standing near the main door. They smiled warmly at me.

"Hi ma'am, I am the beautician Megha and she is the designer Aarti. Sir sent us for you. So we may please come in." She asked as I was staring and smiling at them without blinking.

"Sorry, Hi Megha and Aarti. I am Nikshitra. Please come in. Do you want any drinks like tea or coffee?" I asked them politely but they returned me a smile refusing.

"Thank you. We dont have much time so we will start directly and after that we can have your pleasantries ma'am." Aarti said, smiling towards me. I think both their ages must be in their late twenties.

They have done my hair and eyebrows. The makeup is natural as I don't like my face caked up with makeup. I am brownish and I have to thank god for giving me smooth skin without pimples. But I am insecure about my colour. I have gained confidence because of Ayush.

"Sir has selected this dress for you ma'am. It is nice and beautiful. He has nice taste in selecting clothes." Aarti said to me, smiling. I am feeling proud of my husband for selecting this beautiful dress which fitted me perfectly. It is a long red netted frock with floral pattern and long sleeves. It is an off shoulder dress. But I liked it. I never wore sleeveless. I wore and came out of the closet twirling around feeling happy. I stood in front of the mirror and wore my small mangalsutra and sindoor on my head.

"You are looking beautiful maam." They both said at the same time.

"Thank you." I smiled in return. They went after the work was done saying goodbye to me.

I was waiting for the car. At 6:45pm the driver came. I went and sat in the car imagining what he would say to me. Whether he will complement me or not. I was nervous as hell fidgeting my fingers and rubbing my both hands on the dress as sweat was forming. After 30minutes drive we entered a big hotel. The car door opened revealing my handsome husband standing in front of me looking dashing in his black suit with red bow and hair gelled. I was gawking at him without removing my stance sitting in the car seat. I did not realize when he forwarded his hand towards me. He touched my bare shoulder to come to the real world. I flinched and forwarded my right hand to him.

When I stepped down he was staring at me completely from up to down.

"You look gorgeous. Don't feel nervous. I am there for you." His words did complete magic on me as I am staring at his black

orbs without blinking. Ican see sincerity in him when he complimented me. He held my hand tighter in his when the press came towards us.

"Dont panic. Stick to me and don't go anywhere without informing me." I was shivering in his hold when the press was taking photos of us. I covered my face with my hands as the lights kept blinding me. There were so many people around me and bodyguards were protecting us both to leave the place to move forward.

He held my waist and moved forward not saying anything to them. I embarrassed him in front of the reporters. Is he angry at me? Why am I like this? I can't even stand with him as he is rich and powerful where I am an average middle class girl with not good looks. Tears started to pour from my eyes.

"No, don't feel bad Nikki. Look at me. Look in my eyes." He took me to corner and hugged me close to his chest. He gathered me in my arms rubbing my back to soothe my pain. He lifted my face and looked at me but I looked down not able to see his face. I was disappointed in myself. Why can't I? He calmed me down wiping my tears from my cheeks and kissing both my eyes till my tears stopped. His both hands on my both cheeks rubbing my cheeks with his fingers.

I looked at him when I thought I have to face this situation otherwise his image will be bad.

"Hey Nikki." Sameer came towards us when we were in an awkward position. He turned back when he saw it. Then we have some distance between us being awkward.

"Hello Sameer. How are you?" I rubbed my face with my right palm not showing my vulnerable condition to him.

"I am good Nikki. You are looking very pretty. He is one lucky man to get you." He told me to shift his eyes to Ayush. I can see the smirk on Sameer's face while looking at Ayush.

"She is my wife Sameer. She is lucky to get me." He said, smirking at me. I was shocked at first but I know I am lucky to get him as my husband. How can he say that? Cannot he say he is lucky to get me. No, his ego hurts to say that.

"Hahaha. Let's see. Now move forward all guests are waiting for both of you." We moved forward holding our both hands together, fingers entwining. We both ascended the stairs to get on to the stage. I was looking down as I was not able to face the people around me. Some are whispering and some are glaring at me. I can see so many guests are there and the press is taking both of our photos together.

"Hello ladies and gentlemen. I would like to introduce my wife Nikshitra Ayush Khurana. Please enjoy the night." He hugged me sideways, smiling at me.

Then we met a few of his clients who were gawking at me. I was feeling uncomfortable with their staring but because of Ayush beside me holding my waist tight as if reassuring me it is okay.

All were whispering about me but I don't care about them. Some were bad mouthing about me.

"Low middle class. She got lucky to get the billionaire as her husband. I think she slept with him and got pregnant. That's Why Ayush had married that girl." One girl was discussing nonsense about me in front of other girls. I did not see her face as I was unable to comprehend. I think Ayush also listened to their conversation and he tightened his both fists looking angry as ever. But he did not answer them directly.

"Some whores around here want to make nonsense talk about other lives without living by themselves. I don't know what they think about themselves when they use their mouth to speak." He taunted indirectly and I smiled looking at him. He also smiled looking at my eyes.

"I am hungry Ayush. I will go and eat. You meet them and I am getting bored here. I will come fast." I said to him, Without giving any chance I escaped from there to eat my dinner. I ate all the delicacies present there without caring about anyone. My stomach is full now.

Then I saw a swimming pool arranged with beautiful small lights around. I walked till the edge to see the beautiful surroundings. I was feeling awkward to meet anyone as I am new to this type of world. High and rich class parties are not my thing. I met some clients with Ayush. I only said hello to them without giving any handshake to them.

"Ahhhhhh" As was in my thoughts someone pushed me in the pool. Splash.

Authors note:

Please vote and comment guys if you like this chapter. Slight glimpse of past is shown in this chapter. I will update tomorrow if possible guys.

Embarassed

Authors note:

I am really sorry guys for the late update. I got fever and I was not well for few days. I dont know if I am writing well or not. It is my first time writing a mature content. Please vote and follow me if you like this chapter. Support me guys.

Note: 18+ MATURE CONTENT AHEAD. ---Ayush Pov:

I was conversing with Abhishek who is our new investor in our company. I forgot that Nikki went away for long time. I was checking my watch from time to time as she has gone for long time. We have to go the stage also. I have to introduce her as my wife. I did not went directly because we have arrived early as I want to. I am worried as she is taking so much time to come here when I heard a loud splash and people were gathered around near pool area.

I saw that so many of my guests are seeing towards the pool. When I went passing by them I saw that someone was drowning in the pool. When I saw the dress I recognized it is Nikki. I was shocked for a moment then without a second I jumped into the pool and swam towards her. I gathered her body in my arms and lifted her bridal style. One hand under her calves and another on her waist. I took a moment to breathe and slowly swam towards the edge and placed her on the floor, then I climbed to the floor.

"Nikki, get up. Nikki.. Nikki.. get up." I shaked her shoulders but she was not responding. I was really worried and tears gathered in my eyes as I saw her form. I wiped my face with my hand first and removed the hair which is falling on my forehead. I tapped her cheeks and then checked her breathing by keeping my fingers under her nose. Then I sensed that she was not breathing. I was paralysed for a moment. I checked her heartbeat by keeping my ear near her heart. I think my senses are not working. I can't hear anything. I pressed her stomach with my joining hands a few times. Then I saw that the water was flowing from her mouth. I am relieved for a moment as I can see that she is coughing. I removed my hands from her stomach and directly gathered her in my arms. I hugged her tightly to my chest and kissed on her hair a few times as tears were flowing from my eyes. I was whimpering as I saw her lifeless body a few minutes ago. I thought I lost my family again.

"Ple.ple..ase do..nt eve..rrr do thisss to me again. You know what you are to me. I caaaant live without you Nikki. Please never lea..ve meeee. I don't have anyone." I whimpered when I felt her hands held my torso. I rubbed my palms on her back to ease my worry.

"Ayush. I am fine. Look at me." I slowly unwrapped my arms and looked at her as she opened her eyes and stared at me with love. She slowly moved her hands and held my face with her palms. Without blinking we are staring at each other. Our both eyes are filled with tears and flowing continuously.

"Your eyes became red." She said rubbing with her forefinger under my eye and wiping my tears which are on my cheeks with her thumb.

"I will not leave you Ayush. You get that. If you throw me out of your life also, I will come to you again. I promise you." She said with a smile lingering on her lips as her eyes shined brightly.

I realized that people are watching us fondly. I met my gaze with Sameer who is standing there like he is watching a free show.

"Sameer, take care of the guests and wind up the party." I said to Sameer who is standing there smiling seeing us. I held her in my arms and she slowly stood up from the floor with the help of me. She held my one hand and leaned her forehead on my shoulder. I think she is embarrassed as I can see that she is staring at the ground.

"The party's over guys. You can have your dinner and leave. Thank you for attending and sorry for the inconvenience." Without wasting my time I announced who all had surrounded us and left from there with Nikki. We were walking from the hotel but Nikki held my hand tightly as If she wanted to say something.

I looked towards her and moved aside to see her. She slowly lifted her face and stared directly towards my eyes.

"Can we stay in this hotel? I am feeling uncomfortable in these wet clothes." She awkwardly blinked her eyes several times as if I would say no to her.

"Okay." I said and helped her to sit on the sofa which is near the reception area. I went to the reception and booked a suite for both of us and brought the keys with me.

"Nikki, Shall we go?" I asked her as she is feeling nervous and not lifting her face from the ground. I can see that her face is frozen. She is fidgeting with her fingers continuously and shaking her legs continuously. The dress stuck to her body as her second skin. I can see her curves perfectly through her dress.

She nodded and took my hand which I forwarded for her to take. I kept her close to my body as I can feel that she is very scared. I kept my hand on her waist and we both went to the elevator as all people were looking towards us as if we were some aliens. I did not care about them and directly went to the tenth floor. I hide her in my chest as she is feeling uncomfortable from other people's gazes. I kept my hand on her ear and eyes to avoid seeing her from people's gazes. We slowly walked to our suite and I opened the door with a card. We both entered at the same time as I can feel that she is not leaving my hold. I locked the door and shifted my gaze to Nikki as she was observing her surroundings.

When I was near her I could see that she was controlling her tears which formed in her eyes. One tear escaped from her left eye as I catched it with my forefinger. I took that finger near my lips and kissed it. She is gazing at me emotionally. She burst into tears and started sobbing uncontrollably, hugging me tightly to her body. I was shocked for once as she hugged me putting her whole weight on me.

Due to the sudden collision I unbalanced myself but I held her body firmly towards me as I can't get her to be hurt one more time.

"Nikshu.. It's okay baby. You don't have to feel embarrassed. I know you did not do it intentionally. I am here. Look at me. You don't have to be scared." I patted her head to soothe her but her unstoppable whimpers never came to end. As her sobbing turned into hiccups I lifted her face from my shoulder as I am getting worried for her health. She is not looking at me and her round face became more puffy and her nose became red. She is sniffing as her body is cold.

"Lets get changed." I slowly untangled myself from her body and gathered her face in my hands and said to her to get changed as I can see that she is shivering from the cold. I am also feeling cold but she should get changed and freshen up.

"Go to the bathroom now and freshen up, till then I order a dress for you. Is it okay?" I softly spoke to her as I thought she is feeling uneasy. I left her and took a step ahead to move to make a call but she held my wrist stopping me. I know she doesn't want to be left alone but she may catch a cold and fever due to her wet clothes.

"I am here only. I won't go anywhere leaving you. Okay?" For assurance I blinked my eyes once to know that I am not lying. Then she slowly unwound her hand and left for the bathroom staring at the ground, turning her face several times as If I was there or not to check. I smiled at her actions. As the bathroom door shut I made a call through the landline.

"Hello Sameer. Bring a dress for Nikshitra and for me from nearby. Bring it fast. And I am in the hotel only. The room number is 1005.

Dont be late." I ordered him without listening to his reply. As he said hello I knew he would ask several questions so I hung up without listening to him.

I was sitting on the couch waiting for Nikki to come from the bathroom. I was thinking how all these chaos happened. Whether she slipped into the pool or someone pushed her into the pool. I have to ask her. But I will ask her tomorrow as she is frightened. I was in my thoughts thinking what would have happened if I was late. Thinking about that goosebumps arrived in my skin. Noone was helping her and she should have been careful. I know she is clumsy every time but I can't afford to lose her. I was shocked seeing her lifeless body floating in the pool. It felt like my life has ended. One thing raised in my mind at that time is I have to save her at any cost. My heart stopped for a moment there seeing her in that same position as before when she fell from the stairs. I don't know how many injuries she will get with her clumsiness. I was moving my hair backwards as it is falling in my eyes when the bathroom door opened revealing her.

She was in a bathrobe which reached her knees. I lifted my eyes from bottom to her eyes which are looking down. From top to bottom she is looking cute in the pink bathrobe. I shifted my gaze from her face to her body. Her hair is wet and her bangs are covering her face from her sides. I can see that her robe is not tightened properly as I can see her mid cleavage.

****Mature Content Ahead. 18+ only******

Her hair is covering both sides of neck. When my gaze went towards her breast it became hard. Her nipples are poking out through her robe. Her bathrobe front is deep and I can see her skin with drops of water on it. My mouth opened wide and eyes wide. I can imagine a drool coming out of my mouth looking at her delicious body. It became very hard seeing her only in a bathrobe. One word said from my mind and heart at the same time is Pretty.

"Precious." I said to her going towards her, walking slowly. Each step taken towards her is like a war within me as If I am able to control seeing her. She lifted her face as I said that and gazed at me lovingly and smiled warmly at me. It is a genuine smile I can say when seeing her.

I slowly lifted my one hand and removed her bangs which were falling on her face under her ear. One hand is holding her waist tightly and one palm is touching her cheeks lovingly. With the back of my fingers I rubbed her right cheek and she closed her eyes instantly as if sacouring my touch. Her breathing became harsh and her heart is racing fast as I can feel from her chest which is touching my body. She shuddered under my touch but did not push me away.

"Be mine Nikshitra as of today. I know I told you I will wait but I think I can't wait anymore. Please BE MINE. I will not hurt you. If you tell me to stop, I will stop. Please permit me to be yours?" I requested her as I think I can't control my body anymore. I think my bulge will be visible through my pants. I want to be inside her pussy. I can't wait any longer. I don't want to take cold showers anymore. But if she says no, I will accept it.

"Promise me that you will never cheat on me?" She asked a question pouting cutely with her lips. I can't wait to taste her lips. I want to make her mine today. I want her to forget today's events and make good memories with her.

"I promise you Nikki. I will never cheat you." She should have asked something other than cheating because I can never cheat her.

"I will be yours with my body and soul." She said smiling looking into my eyes which are looking towards her with lust and desire.

I removed my white shirt in a second as I already removed my coat while she was in the bathroom. I kissed her forehead first.

"Thank you." I lifted her bridal style and she hid her face in my chest, shying away. I walked towards the bed and slowly placed her on middle of the bed.

"I will show you what pleasure feels like. If it is hurting you I will stop. It's my promise to you Nikki." I can feel hot in the room with the AC on. I can clearly see her eyes which are scared of me. I know it is new to her. So I slowly started to move my fingers in her wet hair. To make her feel comfortable I leaned towards her side lying on the other side of the bed. She closed her eyes as I slid my fingers in her hair. I bent close to her and kissed her temple and side of her eyes.

I moved forward and kissed her between the eyebrows where she used to keep bindi daily.

"You are beautiful Nikki." I kissed her both eyes taking few minutes not leaving lips from there as I want to savour each moment. My heartbeats raised by each minute by looking at her. My breathing become shallow looking at her divine body underneath me.

I wetted my lips with my tongue as she opened her both eyes looking at me as asking me 'why are you staring at me like that?'. I did not replied to her. I suddenly kissed her lips which are very devouring to me. I bite her lower lip with my teeth as I did not gave her time to respond to it. She was shocked but she gave all the right to dominate her in the kiss. I sucked her lips without wasting a second as my both hands are holding her cheeks and whole weight is on her body. I did not cared at that time as I want to feel her whole body with my touch.

She tried to push me with her hands as she cannot breathe but I held her both hands with my both hands and gathered her hands on the top of her head. I left her lips to let her breathe for sometime. I continued my sloppy kisses towards her chin and jaw.

I pecked her nose and slightly bit it and she laughed merrily. She tried to remove my hold from her hands but I will not leave her today.

"No... you can't leave my hold today. I will hold you forever in my arms." She wriggled under my body but her knee touched my bulge which is under my clothed body and her eyes became wide realizing how hard I am. Her laughing session ended then and there and realized the position we are in.

"Leave my hands Ayush." She requested making a pout with her small pink lips. I pecked her lips and left her hands and held her face one hand under her left ear and another holding her under her waist.

"I want to bite your cheeks Nikki. I love your round round puffy cheeks which are mine. Everytime I look at you I want to bite your cheeks which are soft and smooth." I bit her left cheek without giving her time to analyze. I grazed my teeth on her left cheek slightly and she screamed and pushed me with her hands on my both shoulders. I stopped and looked at her, who was glaring at me.

"Hey.. don't glare because these are mine. I love your cheeks so don't even dare to stop me. Whenever I want I will bite and kiss it. Do you understand?" I rubbed with my thumb where a red colour is forming on her cheek where I was bitten. But I don't feel bad because it is looking so good on her. She is shocked because she opened her mouth widely. I pecked her left cheek to soothe the pain and moved to the right one and she is glaring at me but not stopping me. So I bit her cheek with my teeth lightly and kissed several times to soothe the pain. Her hand is moving at the back of my body feeling breathless. She fists my skin when she feels the pain. Whenever she squeezed my skin with her hands I became harder for her.

"Nikki dont do that. I can't control if you do that. I want to be inside your pussy for a very very long time. You are making it literally hard for me. I will make you feel all the pleasure throughout the night. Don't worry." She closed her eyes feeling my lips going towards her jaw and chin, then her throat. I gave wet kisses throughout her face. I kissed her all the way throughout her throat. Then I slowly shifted her bathrobe from one side of her neck. I can see the mole on the left side of her neck which is small. I kissed the mole as if not to forget it. She breathed hardly as I kissed her several times there without removing my hold from her body.

"This mole is looking perfect and I love it."I spoke while biting where her collarbone and neck meet. She moaned loudly when I bit her there. I slipped her bathrobe from her shoulder and gave kisses there. She also started to kiss me on my shoulder blades when I was kissing her neck. She held me tightly in her arms and gave kisses on my neck and throat. When I bit her she also started to bite me on my neck with her teeth.

A groan escaped my lips when she started to bite me. I stopped my actions and felt the pleasure inside my body and shifted my hard dick towards her core. I opened my mouth to tell her to stop but nothing came out of me.

"Ple...asee stop it otherwise I will take you now only without waiting for another second. I am barely patient with you and you are making it impossible for me to be in control. You can have your way with me other time but now I need you." I held her hair in a fist and stopped her actions midway. I told her face to face without leaving an inch between us, noses touching, eyes full of desire.

I removed the robe knot when she was staring at me and I looked downwards to see her gorgeous body in front of me. She was not wearing anything underneath her robe. Her chest heaving up and down due to laboured breathing. I can't wait to devour her.

--Authors note:

I am really sorry guys for keeping you waiting. If you want next chapter please vote for me. The target is 35 votes. If you like this chapter please vote.

Consummation

Authors Note:

Please guys if you like my story, vote and comment. Please follow me if you like my writing. It is my first time writing a mature chapter. So please forgive me for any mistakes in my writing. If you like this chapter then please vote.

-------**18+ mature content ahead**-----

--Ayush Pov:

While gazing at her naked body, I felt like I was doing wrong for a second when she gazed at me lovingly and kept her eyes down, shying. Then she touched my heart which was beating wildly with her right palm. Then I forgot about the consequences when I saw her eyes which held pure love.

"In my eyes, you are really beautiful. I know in others eyes you look average but for me looks doesn't matter as I recognize your inner soul. I like your habits which attracted me towards you. From morning till evening I know you think of me when I am not there with you. I think not every second you think of me because I know that most of the time you will be on your instagram with your bts. I am really jealous of them. As I am real with you I don't need to worry about them. They cant hold you but I can hold you in my life forever." I said staring directly at her face without blinking to catch her expression while I am expressing my feelings. One tear rolled out of her eyes as she is still not looking at me. Then she opened her eyes fully to see my face.

"I LOVE YOU Ayu." She said only those words while sniffing. Her nose started to water due to her continuous crying. She looked cute while scrunching her nose. She tried to hold her nose with her one hand to stop the phlegm which was ready to come out.

I tried to control my laugh but when she sneezed hiding her full face, I laughed hugging her. After a minute, I slowly removed my arms from her back and tried to held her shoulders while smiling to myself. But she is not removing her hands from her face due to embarassment.

"You don't need to feel embarrassed. I accepted all of you. If I am cold and instead of you if it is my runny nose then will you stay away from me? No na so remove your hands from your face." She slowly removed her hands and looked at me with teary eyes. I gathered the tissues which were at the side table and cleaned her nose, hands and rubbed her face with another tissue which became red due to her crying.

"Thank you for coming into my life. No one has taken care of me except my dad. Now you became one of my family. I thought you think it as gross and will not touch me. So I am controlling my sneeze from long time. But at the correct time it came. What a day for me."

She mocked at last sentence. But I held her face with my both hands and kissed her forehead.

"I wont think like that. You know that but you are insecure about yourself. I will change you in future. If my baby is born and has a cold or fever, should I not take care of them and think it gross and let them be. No, then for your information every inch of you I accept with my whole heart. If you are in any state in this life I will accept you." I said what is there in my heart and kissed her heart with my lips for the very first time in my life closing my eyes savouring the moment.

She held my hair from behind with her one hand and another hand fisting the pillow tightly. She opened her eyes and looked down at me and pulled me up till both of our faces were touching. She kissed my eyes one by one for a minute and kissed my forehead and temple holding my shoulders for support.

"I love you. I love you." She kissed every inch of my face showing her love for me while leaving no gap between us. There is no barrier between us.

"You will always protect me. I know for sure." She pecked my lips holding my face in her both palms. A tear came out of my eyes when she said that and fell on her cheek.

"Dont cry." She said and hugged me tightly, hiding her face on my shoulder and rubbing my back with her soft touches.

Then I realized that our upper bodies are naked and tried to remove myself from her hold. But she is not letting me leave her due to the awkward state we are in.

"I will stop here if you want?" I whispered in her ear. But due to the close proximity she shivered in my hold. As my breath tickled her ear she shifted away from me and looked at the state we are in.

"No. Make me yours today." She said taking my breath away with confidence not feeling awkward.

Slowly I untangled myself and crushed her with my body weight. I got down from the bed and removed my pants on the floor. I am only in boxers. She turned away feeling shy. Then I got up on the bed and pulled her face near me.

"I want you now." I said to her as my body is filled with desire for her.

"I will make love to you and stop me if you feel any pain. Okay?" I kissed her nipples which are so soft and I touched her mounds with my right hand and kissed her mid valley of the breasts. It is so soft and smooth. I want to feel them daily.

"So soft." I kissed her both peaks and touched her stomach which was waiting for me to devour it. I laid my face on her breast which is near her heart listening to her heart beats. Whenever I touch her she shivers. As it is her first she is conscious.

" Ayush, itttt tic..kles. Please stoooopp." She stuttered and giggled while I was giving wet kisses on her belly button holding her waist tightly. But I did not stop as I am feeling ecstatic. I kissed her every inch of the upper part of her body except her private part.

I touched her thighs and she shivered slightly without opening her legs. With my back hand I touched her both thighs while I was sitting near her. I kissed her feet slowly and the anklets which are present on her both legs.

"I love them. Whenever you are near to me, it gives me the signal that you are there near me with that sound. I will buy you many more and don't ever remove them.okay?" She nodded while closing her eyes, fisting the bedsheet in her both hands. I slowly kissed till the end of calves and removed my boxers in a swift move as she was still closing her eyes. I came up face to face and covered both of our bodies with the duvet present on the bed. I know she will be shocked if she sees my dick. As it is long and hard for her. She may get frightened, so for safety I will not show it to her.

"Are you ready?" She nodded looking into my eyes and slowly I placed my right palm on her pussy and she literally looked scared. When I touched her, she started shifting uncomfortably. Her legs are moving so I sat on her to stop her movements.

"It will be okay. Dont worry." Slowly I opened her folds with my fingers looking in her eyes and opened her legs wide to accommodate myself in between her legs. With my left hand I am touching her and with my right hand I hold my dick. I slowly rubbed my tip on her clit which was wet. She is wet for me. I can sense that she is feeling so many euphoric emotions by looking in her eyes. I slowly rubbed my shaft in between her folds and I tried to enter my tip in her vagina.

"It is so tight Nikki. I am so hard for you Nikki." I closed my eyes, unable to control myself and entered her slowly, hiding my face on her shoulder. Half way through I opened my eyes and saw her breathing heavily controlling her tears. Her eyes were wide open and held my back with both hands hugging me tightly, not leaving an inch gap between us. My breaths became shallow and rubbed her tears with my right hand and held her waist with my other hand.

Her walls seem to be tight so I entered forcefully breaking her hymen. She screamed loudly scratching my back with her nails and I can sense blood dripping from her vagina. I did not move. So I stayed in that position till it got adjusted.

"I love you." I said and kissed her tears which were flowing uncontrollably. I kissed her full face and made patterns on her breast without removing myself from her. I started to kiss her left breast and slowly removed my shaft till the tip and again I entered her not giving any time to feel the pain. I started to thrust her deeply till the end of her vagina.

"Ah.. please... Please.." She begged for her release. Slowly her pain started to fade and started to feel ecstatic. She started to move her hips along with me when I thrust her slow.

"Please what Nikki?" I started to thrust her hard and slow while kissing her neck and biting her mole.

"Mo..ve fasterrrr ple..please. I can't." She came while I was still thrusting her in and out of her vagina. She started to breath heavily as her orgasm hit her and sweat trickled down from both of our bodies. I held her both hands and joined them with both my hands and stared at her eyes which were ready to droop. I kissed her fingers while thrusting her.

I rubbed her clit with my thumb and the sound of slapping our bodies made me move faster in her. I am very close to cumming, my dick got swollen and throbbing in pain to release.

"Look into my eyes Nikshu. Cum when I tell you. Okay?" I started thrusting wildly in her and released my seeds in her, hitting her g spot and she came. I am breathing heavily and did not remove my shaft from her. I slowly removed my face from her chest and looked at her who was close to drifting to sleep.

"Now is the punishment as you did not listen to me." I gazed into her eyes to see the reaction. And her eyes opened wide when she reached her senses and got the meaning of my words.

"No. Now stop." She said frantically after reaching her heights of pleasure.

"I am still hard for you. You will have to pay for all the cold showers I have taken in my life because of you". I said grinning and her eyes and mouth opened widely in shock.

---Authors note:

If you guys want next update then the target is 35 votes. I have published this chapter because of your request guys. Last chapter as not completed my target votes but still due to the request of readers I published this chapter. Please guys vote this chapter and I will update fast.

Authors note

Today is my birthday guys. So I will write a chapter for you. Maybe till today night. Follow me guys

Revenge

Ayush Pov:

The morning rays fell on my face, I rubbed my eyes to remove the tiredness which I am feeling. I tried to get up then I saw Nikki sleeping on my torso. Then I remembered what had happened at night.

Then I felt disgusted with myself.

"how can I do this with her? What will she think? I know I shouldn't have done that. But I did not have control last night. My mom will be ashamed of me."

With this thought I moved my hair backwards which is falling on my forehead. I gripped my hair tightly as I am feeling bad.

"I have to think of a solution. I know from the start that I have to do this with her, then only my revenge will succeed. She totally deserves it. But I did not think it would be this fast. From today onwards she will see a different side of me. The game of revenge begins. You will think 'why am I alive' from now onwards."

With this thought I slowly held her head which was on my stomach and placed her on the bed and went to the bathroom naked to wash myself.

While I was looking at myself in the mirror, I remembered her screaming my name with lust. Those eyes which have so much love and trust on me, make me want to take her again and again at that time. I did take her 4 times after the first time. I did not have control of myself at that time as she is very beautiful and naked, like asking me to devour her with her eyes which held pure lust and love for me. Her moans and her pussy made me hard for her. I cannot forget her face which held pure emotions reflecting on her face.

"Why?Whyyy? Whyyy did you do this to me? Why am I feeling regret? Why should I feel remorse?No, You deserve it? You deserve it for what you have done. You made my world crumble with your innocence. But I know 'what are you'. I will make your life hell. NOW THE GAME BEGINS." With this a lone tear escaped from my eye and I punched the mirror with my right fist not able to control the anger within me.

While taking a bath, I rubbed my body vigorously to remove the touch of her from my body. My body became red with continuous scratching and rubbing. At my back I could feel her nail scratches so I tried to rub hard and small drops of blood flowed, so I stopped myself. I took the towel and tied it to my waist. I took another towel to dry the water from my body.

I wore last night clothes which are away from the bed and at each corner of the room. I didn't want to look at her, so I avoided and went towards the dressing room to make myself presentable.

While opening the door, due to the disturbance she shifted and rubbed her eyes while scrunching her nose and woke up. She dont know that she was naked. So with her palms she is rubbing her face. Slowly she got up and the bedsheet fell from her upper part of the body, which I have covered to not think about her body. But she has to make it difficult for me. I can see the red marks which have been gifted by me. My love bites and her both tits are tempting me to take her again in pure bliss.

"No,No, Keep your mind off the gutter Ayush." I mumbled to myself and closed my eyes to keep calm.

"Good morning Ayush, where are you going?" I grit my teeth when she smiled towards me and forgot to cover herself.

"Cover yourself if you want to walk yourself." I gritted my teeth and said to her then she realized she was naked. She hurriedly took the bed sheet to cover her upper part and closed her eyes and opened her mouth due to embarrassment.

"I will wait in the lobby. Wash yourself and come. " I spoke harshly and went out by banging the door shut loudly. I walked fast to avoid her. I don't know what I will do to her.

Nikshitra Pov:

"What happened to him? Why he is behaving harshly? I think it may be office problem. I will talk to him after going to our home." I spoke to myself after he went out.

Then I remembered yesterday night. All events are running in my mind making me shy and to close my eyes with my palms. How he made love to me, how I felt pure love in his each and every action. He showed me what pleasure is. I can still feel goosebumps all over my body wherever he touches me. I felt alive after he made me his. I am smiling remembering how he kissed me all over my body when I felt tired after our love making. He kept telling me his love throughout the night with his actions. I did not sleep well as he took me 5 times. I was very tired but he was insatiable. It was our first time, so he did not control himself. I am very lucky to have him as my husband.

I hit my head twice to stop smiling and thinking about last night's events. It was a memorable night for me. I think my life will be blissful if Ayush loves me throughout my life. I don't know what my life would be like if he was not there in my life. If he changes also, I can love him. I will change according to him.

With this thought, I slowly managed to get down from the bed with the bedsheet around me. When I kept both my legs on the floor, I felt an unbearable pain to stand on the ground. My lower part is hurting so much. I felt tears in my eyes as I wasn't able to walk. Taking slow steps I went to the bathroom and saw that the mirror was broken.

"Who broke the mirror?", I questioned to noone as I was thinking it may be from an accident from Ayush. As I know yesterday it was good. I think something may have fallen on the mirror so it is broken. The pieces are on the washbasin slab and some pieces have fallen on the floor.

Without getting hurt, I picked each and every piece and threw it in the dustbin. I can see myself in the broken mirror that my face is glowing. I can see each and every mark he marked on me. It has turned bright red. I can see his artwork on my neck and on my stomach.

While showering I can see the dried blood flowing down from my vagina and inner thighs. I slowly rubbed my body with soap and dried myself with the towel and went out of the bathroom and wore the clothes which were brought yesterday. It is a beautiful cotton dress with half sleeves with flower patterns on it. It is covered till my ankles so I don't need to worry. I am insecure to show my body to others, as I think I am dark skinned and I can't wear revealing clothes. If like last night anybody taunts or embarasses me then I cant able to defend myself. Then I dried my hair with the towel and removed the bed sheets and threw it in the laundry basket. The blood marks are there on the bed sheet so I removed them. After getting ready in the dressing room, I went out taking my belongings with me.

After seeing me without speaking a word, Ayush got up and straightly walked to the entrance of the hotel and sat in the driver seat of his car which is brought by the valet. He did not even glance at me. I was shocked by his behaviour, I practically matched his steps. I was looking at him while he sat in the car. He blew the car horn, then I came out of my thoughts and opened the car door and sat in the passenger seat without wasting any time.

"Ha..Ha..", I cleared my throat to grab his attention, but he was not even blinking. He started to drive the car. I tried to talk with him but he is not even responding to me. The car driver went in silence without any spoken words.

When we reached our mansion, without uttering any word he went and opened the main door and walked to the main hall without looking back. I was confused by his actions. I got down and slowly walked towards him, who was sitting on the sofa with head down and both hands tightly fisted. I can't even see his face. I don't know what he is thinking. So I touched his shoulder with my right hand.

"Ayush, What happened?", Without a second he pushed me with his right hand. In shock I fell down on the floor. When I touched him, he pushed my hand.

"DON'T TOUCH ME YOU BITCH.", He shouted loudly with angry orbs and bloodshot eyes, he showed his palm in front of my face while standing up. His whole demeanour changed and shivering in anger, gritting his teeth making my whole body to shiver. I was shocked and tried to talk with him.

"What is the problem Ayush? Why are you behaving like this? Why are you calling me bitch?", I calmly asked him as I don't know what happened. I can't behave irrationally. It may be an office problem. He may be in tension, that's why he is behaving like this. I was compromising myself that he may be in trouble.

But I don't know that it is my biggest mistake in my life. From now on I did not even think that my life became hell.

"You are my problem. You Idiot. You don't even know that I am acting. The plan is a success. I took your virginity. I made you mine but I forgot to tell you one thing. Tsk..tsk..tsk..that is I married you for my REVENGE." He smirked at me while smiling and his eyes showing hate towards me. Nothing but anger in his whole demeanour.

"You ugly bitch. Look at your body. No one will look at you for even once. Can you imagine I was the one who sacrificed ny virginity to you. I am feeling like all insects are running on my skin after touching you. Looking at your face, noone wants to live with you. You are a hypocrite who does not even defend yourself when others blame you. Look in the mirror and thank me for marrying you. Noone will marry you after seeing your face. I married you to make your life hell. Now welcome to hell 'my ugly wife'." He grabbed my hair and we are both face to face while he spoke harsh words. I can't even imagine that he is acting. I am shocked to the core.

"No..No..No.. you are lying. I k..know youuuu. Youuu ar..rere no..t acting. I know that you are a very good per..son. You can't betray me. I know you." I shuttered while tears were flowing from my eyes. I was on the floor not able to handle the situation. He fisted my hair tightly, glaring at me to stop my nonsense. But I am not backing off. I know there may be a reason for his action. I know he is not telling the truth. His love, his concern towards me is not acting. I can feel his care and concern.

I shake my head not realising that he raised his hand towards me. My head turned right side and cheek is throbbing in pain. I was beyond shocked.

"What happened to you? Why are you lying to me? The concern and care you showed towards me is also a lie. I don't believe you. You are my Ayush. You are lying..lying..LYING." I shouted at him loudly and another hard smack which made my body fall to the floor.

"Don't believe my words. But you can believe my actions right. So I will show you how you do not believe. I hate you Nikshitra. I really hate you. I can't even imagine how I managed to live with you. I have to show your ugly slut face as my wife to everyone. You disgust me. While touching you, I feel like puking. You are a useless creature. Don't even know what people feel about you." I was angry while he was speaking ill about me. He is degrading me. How can he? Is it the truth of my life? He is acting and I didnt even know that. What a fool I became. I should not have believed him. That is the biggest mistake of my life. Atlast I felt betrayed.

---Authors note:

I am really sorry guys for the late update. It is short update and I will try to update the next chapter long. Thank you for all your warm wishes. I want to update on my bday but I could not. So sorry guys. I was busy. I will try to update two times in a month. So please read and vote the chapter, if you like it. Please follow me guys. Thank you and vote this chapter if you want next update. I will update if the target is 40votes guys. So please vote

Defying him

Nikshitra Pov:

"Why are you doing this to me? Why did you slap me? I didn't even make any mistakes. What revenge are you speaking of? I didn't even know you before your marriage proposal. I know there might be a misunderstanding. So please don't speak harsh words with me. Don't degrade me with those names. You also know that I am not a bitch as YOU ARE THE ONE WHO TOOK MY VIRGINITY. DON'T FORGET THAT." I shouted at him at last, holding his arms tightly, standing myself on the ground, glaring at him for speaking nonsense with me, continuously tears flowing from my eyes. I will also not sit silent if he thinks I will bear all his accusations. No NEVER. I will also see till how many days this hate will be there in his eyes.

His jaw clenched while I spoke to him without fear. Closing his eyes for a second, he opened his eyes and glared at me with bloodshot eyes, nothing but hate can be seen in his eyes for me. He tightly gripped my hands and pushed me from him. I stumbled but I held myself in time without falling.

"Okay then, as you said I will show you what the hell means. You are not getting what I told you. So be in your world of imaginations. From now onwards YOU ARE NOT MY WIFE. DO YOU GET IT?", He shouted loudly and his voice echoed all over the mansion and I flinched at his voice. But I kept my stand. I narrowed my eyes at him for saying that I am not his wife.

"No, I don't believe you. I know you love me. There might be a misunderstanding. Please listen to me. You care for me. I have seen your love towards me. I can't believe your words, but I see it in your actions since our marriage. So I know you love me.If you want me to leave you, then I am telling you, I will never leave you, not in this life. It is my promise. 'YOU ARE MY HUSBAND, DO YOU GET THAT' not even in this life you will make me get away from your life.", I shouted at him similarly and grabbed his collar with both hands without any fear and glared at his eyes to defy me. I will not backoff, if he thinks that he can do whatever he wants. I am not a slave to him to listen to him.

" I will not listen to you. Do whatever you want? I don't care. I trusted you the most after my dad. So I believe in my love and you believe whatever you think. I will not prove to you that I am telling the truth, AYUSH KHURANA. So go and believe all lies which have been said about me. I will never give any explanation to you IDIOT." He was astounded by my reply with wide eyes and open mouth. After a minute, he came back to his senses and he was looking at me deeply with a frown with gritting teeth.

He tried to remove my hold from his collar, but I never budge. So at last he tightly held my wrist and it started to hurt so much. If I did not remove he may break my hand. So I slowly removed not blinking my eyes even for a second and my tears were flowing uncontrollably from both of my eyes. In anger I also pushed him on his both shoulders after removing my hands from him. He stumbled but managed himself and raised his hand to slap me, but I stopped by holding his wrist which was about to touch my cheek.

"Let go of my hand, YOU BITCH. I will kill you. I hate you so much that I never want to see your face. But I will take my revenge from you and I will make sure that you want to kill yourself. Be ready to face the consequences of what you have done." He removed his hand from my hold and pointed his forefinger and threatened me. But I will also see What he does to me. Her replies made him more furious.

"If I am a bitch, why did you sleep with me? OHOH, I forgot that you are also a virgin. Tsk..Tsk..Tsk you lost to this bitch only. I feel great that you have lost it to me. You are a used product like me. If you call me again with these useless names, then I will also show what I am.", She smirked and pointed her forefinger at his heart while giving her comebacks to the glaring man who was standing surprised at her different behaviour.

"Ok you are nothing but useless to me. So if you are living in my house you have to follow my rules. You have to obey my orders to stay in this house. You are not even working. All the time crying, crying. You can't even do a single task without trouble. So from now onwards you will work as my slave. Now 'WELCOME TO MY BEAUTIFUL WORLD DARLING'", He taunted me while smirking and smiling showing his teeth. I want to punch him left and right. I know I don't have a job as of now. I do only house chores. He does not have to say it in my face that I am not earning money.

"Ok I will give you the rent for living in your house. I will look for a job and my expenses will be taken care of. I..", he stopped me with his palm while I was talking to him and what he said made me more furious than before.

"Na.Naa. From now on, you cannot go outside this mansion. You only said that you will not leave me in this life, so you cannot even keep a foot outside this mansion. Your mobile and all the belongings which are given by me will be taken. And You will listen to me without asking any questions. Is that clear?" He smiles and smirks looking at me with hate, folding his hands below his chest. As if he is enjoying this drama, I want to kill him with my bare hands. I closed my eyes for a second to keep my anger at bay. I will say in his language only then he will understand my words.

"No, I will not listen to you. Who are you to dictate to me? You only said na 'YOU ARE NOT MY WIFE.' I will not work for you." I quoted his words imitating him with my hands smiling to myself as if I won an award. His jaw clenched and my words and smile made him more furious. He tightly fisted his both palms on his sides as I am not backing down. He thinks that I will listen to whatever he says. No, Never. I patted myself in my mind as I defied him.

"Okay. You will not listen to me? One last time I am asking 'Will you listen to me or not?' If not.." I shake my head left to right as indicating NO while he glared as if he wants to kill me now and there itself. I folded my hands smirking to myself but I did not expect the outcome of my anger.

Then, he suddenly held my both hands and lifted me on his shoulder like a sack and walked fast to somewhere I don't know. I was frightened for a minute and came back to my senses. My face and half of the body upside down, I was shocked at his behaviour.

"Let go. Let go, you rascal. Let go of me. What will you get? Leave me youuuuu. Leave me. Why are you doing this? Where are you taking me?" I continuously beat on his back with both hands while I cried the whole way. I don't know where he is taking me. I am afraid. What will he do to me? No..No.. Will he rape me? No. I can't let that happen. Where is he taking me? With the sudden realization, my hands started to shiver. My whole body got frightened of the outcomes. But he never replied back. As I can't see his face, I tried to gain his attention by pinching on his back but he did not even give any reaction. He did not even stop for once as he fastly walked.

When I saw the surroundings, I knew where he was taking me. It is my old room which is a store room. 'What have I got myself into?' I slapped my forehead with my palm scrunching my nose and frown marring my forehead.

"This is your room from now on. Now enjoy your life and be ready for your punishment for not listening to me. You will face the real side of me and you will fear me. I can guarantee that. Enjoy 'MY

UGLY WIFE'. No one will give you food till you listen and obey my orders. When you say YES, then only you get your food.", He dropped me on the floor after opening the door and he stood tall and smirked seeing me on the floor. I tried to get up but I felt dizzy as I have not even eaten the food since morning. He shut the door without even listening to my answer, as he knows that I will never accept his conditions.

Good for him. What does he think of himself? Is he a king that I should obey his orders? Go fuck Yourself Idiot. I will never listen to him. He has to bear the consequences of slapping me. He slapped me twice. I will never forget that. After marriage I forgave him thinking it may be a misunderstanding. But NO. He has to gain hard for my forgiveness. No one has slapped me in my life. He is the one who slapped me. I know I am a girl with average looks. But he cannot degrade my character. I am not beautiful but he married me saying he liked me. Why does he always lie? What will he gain? Nothing. He is thinking that I have done something to him. I didn't even know him before.

I gathered myself thinking all has happened before and got up holding my head and went to the small bathroom which was present in the room. I took slow steps as my lower part is still in pain and my body is aching so much. I washed my face to remove the dizziness and tiredness from my face.

"I don't know what is happening in my life. Whom should I trust? Whom should I not? He is so confusing. One day he will show all the love he has and next he acts like he hates me from the bottom of his heart. He is bipolar, I can conclude that. But I don't know why he changed in one night. What has happened? Is he really telling the truth? Is this all acting? He never loved me? No.. No.. I can see it in his eyes that he loves me. I will make him realize that. That is for sure." I spoke to myself in the mirror and asked the questions which were running in my mind. My eyes became red and puffy due to continuous crying and my face is also swollen. My lips are chapped as I did not even drink a drop of water. I washed my face with soap and dried my face with the towel present there, which I have not used for so many days. As no one is living in this room since I went to his room. I don't want to think about anything as of now. I want to avoid that he did not love me. I can't imagine my life without him. Then how can I bear the thought of not being loved by him?

Will He really does not give me food? I have been hungry since morning. I did not eat anything. My stomach is grumbling due to hunger.

I sat down on the floor my back facing the wall and bought my legs to my chest and interwining my both hands and rested them on my knees thinking about my future.

"It may be some misunderstanding. When he realizes his mistake. He will come to me and apologise to me. I know him. Whenever he makes a mistake he will apologise. I will play hard this time. I will not forgive him easily." With this thought I slept on the cold floor without any blanket or pillow as I was very tired. I did not think that this is the imagination I am living in this world. I did not know that my life will change from tonight.

--Authors note:

Thank you guys who all have voted for me. It will be interesting from next chapters. I apologise for any grammatical mistakes. If you like this chapter please click the star mark below. How is the chapter. Please comment below. Please follow me.

Hungry

Ayush Pov:

"What is wrong with me? Why am I thinking about her? She never listens to me. What should I do to forget her even for one day. She is really getting on my nerves." I banged both fists on my office table thinking about her. I have to do something as she will obey my orders from now on otherwise she will bear the punishments which she cannot bear.

I came directly to the office after locking her in the storeroom. I really want to live happily with her. But we cannot change the past and the mistakes or sins in my language are done. It is irreparable. I want to divorce her and humiliate her in front of the world. But I can't leave her. I don't know what I would do if she left me. The thought only is devastating me as I am getting addicted to her as I am living a lonely life. I am giving priority to her and I know it is wrong to think like that.

I smiled remembering when she is fiesty and glaring at me with her beautiful eyes which tell her innocence. I regret slapping her with my hand. I want to punch myself for manhandling her but I have to do this for my peace. I will pay for my sins. I know that but first she has to pay for her deeds. It is the most beautiful night for me remembering her body beneath me which has pure emotions. I did not even eat food as she also did not eat. I can't even bring myself to eat after treating her badly. I can't think how she is bearing her hunger as she is a foodie. I only drank water to hydrate myself. I can't even concentrate on my work because of her as she is in my mind 24 hours. I have signed the last file and called my PA Mythri.

"Pack up and schedule my meetings tomorrow which I missed and prepare all the files which are needed and send the soft copy to me. I will sign the remaining files tomorrow." I said in my hard tone and stood up to leave my office. Now it is evening 7pm. I have to go to my home to check on her whether she is doing any drama or not.

She is really a sick baby and always causes trouble. I don't want to give her food till she listens to me but I don't even know if I can be patient till that time. Whenever she gets sick I move forward to help her as I cannot see her like that. My heart hurts when she is hurt or crying.

I hopped in my Audi and drove fast without waiting. I opened the main door with the keys as I reached in 30minutes. I went directly to the store room to check on her. She is sleeping soundly on the floor as she did not sleep yesterday. I moved forward and touched her forehead with my back hand and my gaze turned to her red cheek which was swollen due to my evilness. I want to slap myself for beating her. I slowly moved my palm from her forehead to her cheek and felt warm and her breathing was normal. She slightly stirred in her sleep due to an uncomfortable position. I backed away and thought she might wake up by my touch and moved away and slowly shut the door and went to my room without looking back as I know I can't control while looking at her.

Her face reminds me of her purity and innocence. She might be dark skinned but I like her nature which is selfless and childish. She doesn't even think of herself while helping others. She does not care who taunts her. She feels hurt but never talks back. She opens up only to her close people and shows her true nature. She defends herself in front of her people only not others. She is unique and I live about her. She likes clothes but not expensive ones which are affordable to her. She doesn't like revealing clothes and is insecure about her colour.

One has to live with them to know the character of them; neither their face nor body can show the character. I think like that. I know I have called her names to degrade her to know I hate her.

I freshen up in my room and wore my pyjamas. I tried to sleep but a frown was marring my face thinking about her. I was slightly dizzy due to not eating food. My stomach is continuously growling but I can't even eat the food as she is also hungry. I rolled in my bed but I couldn't even sleep. I shifted sides but I can't sleep as I am addicted to her cuddling. I want to sleep. Without her I can't even sleep. I put the pillow on my face to not think what will I do if I remain here for some more time.

"I won't, I won't. I will not go to her. Ayush don't think about her. You have to go to office tomorrow. Sleep without any thoughts. She us not here so think how you hate her. Think about what crime she did. You can't feel about her. Get that in your head." I talked to myself banging my face with the pillow tightly closing my eyes.

"This one time I will go to her. It is my promise to myself." I thought and sprang to her room to sleep. I took my pillow and bed sheet, slowly entered her room. Arranging the pillow beside her pillow I made a space for myself in that tiny room. I gazed at her loving face which adorned with smile and frown etched on her face. She is sleeping hugging herself as she is not covered with any blanket. I took hold of my blanket and covered her. I held her hand which was lying freely and I traced her hand and intertwined them. The soft touch of her ignited several emotions within me. I took her hand and placed a kiss on the back of her palm.

"I am really sorry for behaving like that with you. But I can't help it. I have to do this to give justice. Then only I can move on. After breaking you, I will amend my mistakes and it is my promise to you." One tear left my eye as I looked at her serene face which held longing and love for me.

I kissed her finger tip and placed a long kiss on her palm. I slowly moved forward and grabbed her waist and her head landed on my chest. I caressed her hair to not disturb her sleep and pecked her temple before going to sleep. I tightly hugged her to myself and drowned in my sleep.

Next morning:

When I got up Nivi was sleeping soundly on my chest. Drool left her mouth and her mouth open, snoring lightly. I smiled looking at her. I slowly lifted her face from myself and placed her head on the pillow and covered her with the blanket. I moved forward slowly not making any sound and shut the door lightly and locked it.

"Who is that? Ayush? Are you there? Please open the door. Open it. Open the fucking damn door. Otherwise I will kill you. Are you opening or not? I know you are listening. Open the damn door you IDIOT." I was surprised at her cursing and actions. How she knows that I am here only.

"I won't open the door. When you listen and follow my rules then only I will open this door. Do you get that?" I made my heart stone as she will not give up easily. I know her, without fighting she never gives up.

"Okay don't open the door. I will not listen to you. Go to hell. What do you think of yourself? Are you the Prime minister of India listening to you? I will die of hunger but I will not obey you. Get that in your head." She shouted at me and I was shocked at her words. I thought she could never bear her hunger. But I was wrong. She was taunting me but I smiled as she was shouting. She looks cute while giving taunts in anger.

"I will go to hell. Thank you for telling me. Bye bye, enjoy your morning. I am making my breakfast. I will eat a healthy breakfast today as I am so happy. Bye Bye. Good morning darling." I also shouted and walked past the room.

It is early in the morning. So I decided to freshen up and got ready to make my breakfast which consists of chapathi, puri and aloo curry. I know she likes Indian food so I prepared it myself. It took 1hr to complete the task in hand. I took it to her room so she gets tempted and gives up her attitude.

"Nikki, Are you there? I brought my breakfast. I prepared puri and chapati. If you want you can come outside and eat it but on one condition that is you will follow my rules." I talked nicely and smiled mischievously thinking about her face when food is there in front of her. It is her favourite. She cannot miss it. I know that.

"No, I wont eat. I am not hungry. You eat it. It is your own house. I am none to you for you to care. So enjoy your food Ayuuuuush." She said in the same way I spoke to her.

"Ok, thank god I thought you would ask for breakfast. I made it only for one person. So thank you for sparing me. I will eat this delicious food myself. Mmmh Mmmh. It is so good. I love this. I think God gifted me these hands to make food for myself. It is so delicious.MmhMmh " I moaned and started eating by myself as I was famished. I was hungry yesterday as I did not eat food. I want to know till how much time she will bear her hunger.

A knock on the door interrupted my eating session. I left the plate there and washed my hands and went to see who will visit in the early morning.

"Wait. Don't knock continuously." I said to the one who is knocking continuously that I hate it.

"Sameer. What are you doing here early in the morning?" I was surprised to see him without answering me. He entered the living room and sat on the sofa.

"I smell food. What did Nikki make? I am hungry. Please give me food." He made a puppy face, avoiding my question. I sighed and went to the kitchen to bring food for him.

"Come to the dining table and eat." I said moving forward his plate but that idiot sat on the sofa in indian style and started to devour his food like he was dying without food for so many days.

"Some people dont change." I twitched my lips seeing him as he is like that only.

"Where is Nikki? She is nowhere to be seen. What is she doing?" He asked several questions at a time with his mouth full of food. I understood as he is my long time friend.

I don't know what to answer him. I shifted in my seat uncomfortably and avoided his eyes to answer him as he could catch my lie.

"She is.." A continuous banging interrupted my talking as I could hear her shouting. I banged my head with my hand and I know what will be the situation afterwards. He looked towards me and upwards to know what was happening. He will create havoc now. She can escape now that Sameer is here. He will side with her forgetting me.

"What is happening? Where is Nikki? You didn't even answer me. Why is Nikki shouting? Tell me." He glared towards me and gripped his fists tightly, forgetting his food which is kept on a teapoy now. I kept silent as I know he may punch me for caging her.

"I will go and check. Why is she banging? You have to answer me Ayush without telling any lie." He groaned and left upstairs to the room where the sound was coming. I went after him to clear his doubts. Nikki can say anything to him. She may tell the truth of our relationship. With that fear in my mind I moved forward and my face became nervous thinking about the consequences. Sameer is my best friend, I don't want him to leave me alone.

"Help, HELP. Is there anyone? Please help me." She is shouting continuously as I was feeling agitated with her noise. He glared at me and tried to open the door but it was locked.

"Sameer, Is that you? Thank god. Please open this door." She requested him and he turned fully towards me and folded his hands below his chest looking angry. His face contorted with rage and fury.

"Give me the keys NOW. I will deal with you later." He growled in front of me and I shook my head not giving into him.

"No, I will not give it. It is my personal matter. You don't have to be involved in it, Sameer. I have the reason to lick her up in the store room. You don't understand. So let it be Sameer." I tried to explain to him but who is he to listen to me. He never listens and everytime he defies me the same as Nikshitra.

"If you will not give me the keys then I will never enter in your house ever." He threatened me and I Was shocked at his outburst and I gave him the keys, sighing dejectedly. I know he may be serious by looking at his face. So I gave him the keys taking it from my pants pocket.

He unlocked the door fast and Nikki jumped in front of him breathing heavily.

"Thank you very much Sameer Bhaiya. Thank you, thank you. You don't know how much I am grateful to you. I will never forget this help." She smiled at him and dashed towards the kitchen running fastly skipping the stairs one at a time.

We both were shocked at her speed and I went towards the kitchen avoiding him. She sat on the dining table and ate the food without caring about anyone. She did not even spare me a glance and sat in indian style like Sameer in the chair. I don't know what is wrong with them. I cant even take the plate from her as Sameer is watching both of us continuously to answer what is happening.

--Authors note:

Please vote and comment if you like this chapter.

Basement

Nikshitra Pov:

"Sameer bhaiya Did you have your breakfast?" While eating I gazed only at Sameer bhaiya who was standing in shock. After a few seconds he closed his mouth coming out of the shock.

"Yeah I had my breakfast. You eat first. Why did that idiot lock you in the room? Tell me I will take care of it if he does any wrong to you. I will kick him in the ass." He sat beside my chair and patted my head with his one hand. He looked at me with adoration and I smiled seeing him turn towards Ayush glaring at him.

"It is a small issue bhaiya. He got angry and locked me in the store room. I can deal with it. If I can't deal with it then I will ask for your help. Please I can't say more than that. Thank you bhaiya for being here with me." I was emotional looking at bhaiya. I thought of telling him how his dear friend treated me yesterday. But I can't involve third person in our matters. It will get more complicated. Their friendship might get destroyed because of me.

Ayush has no one except me and Sameer. So I have to think carefully before saying anything to Sameer. Sameer bhaiya's phone rang disturbing my thoughts.

"Hello, yeah I am coming." He picked up the call and after speaking for a second he hung up. I was staring at Sameer not even glancing at my husband as he is the one who is the cause of my miseries.

"Nikki, I have an urgent meeting and I have to go. If you have any problem, don't hesitate to call me. If he is the reason for your tears I will see to it that he can't even see your face until he kneels and begs in front of me to see you." He threatened Ayush while glaring and he wanted to tell what will happen if anything happens to me. I was grinning ear to ear that I have my brother if I had any problem and he will help me. I know that for sure. I sat feeling sad while he left without saying any goodbye.

I was ready to leave to wash my hands then suddenly I was jerked back with a palm which holded my wrist and collided with his chest. I was startled and stared wide eyed at him.

"What was that?" He menacingly shouted at me with his booming voice. I was shocked and tried to get out of his grip. He held my waist with one hand from back and another held my wrist. I started wiggling in his hold not even looking at him after what he did with me. I don't want to see his face as of now.

" Leave me. Get the fuck off me." I shouted in the same tone as him as I am not afraid of him.

"Curse one more time in front of me. You will bear the punishment Nikki." He threatened me but I did not back off and glared at him looking in his eyes. He can do whatever he wants. I will not back off. I did not stop my wiggling but that my namesake husband tightened his hold on me.

"What more can you do Mr Ayush Khurana. I HATE YOU. FUCK OFF." I shouted at him and he looked 10 times more dangerous than yesterday. He dug his nails on my wrist. I know blood may be oozing out and bruises may be formed but I will not let any tear fall and wont show any signs of pain in front of him.

He gritted his teeth in anger and left my hold on my waist. He dragged me outside of the house with him walking fast. Not walking fast, it is called running without sparing me a glance. Not even turning back he opened the garage. I started to get fear of what he might do with me.

"Leave me. I am sorry. Please leave me. I am really sorry Ayush. Please I beg you to leave me." He opened the basement room which is located in the garage. I was shocked and started begging him to leave me. But he did not even hear my single request.

I tried to get out of his hold by pinching him and I sat on the floor not moving an inch and he turned back and was very much furious by seeing his face. I cried and begged him.

"You don't understand what I say to you. I will get my revenge. So I know what to do with you. You always make me angry. Now I will see how much more confidence you have." He said and held both of my shoulders and stood me up straight and I was shocked listening to his words. I don't know what will be there in the basement room.

I was feeling numb and my tears were continuously flowing through my eyes and whimpers left my mouth.

"No..No.. don't leave me in this room. I am sorry. Please.. please.." I fell down and held his legs with both my hands and my face burying at his legs while continuously apologising.

He lifted me with both hands and I stood straight. My face contorted with pain seeing the opening of the basement. I am frightened to the core.

"I will do whatever you say. Please don't lock me in this room." I held my both hands in front of him as I was not getting any good vibes seeing the passageway.

" I told you many times but you did not even listen to me. So you will know what will happen if you do not obey me. Today Sameer was there to help you but from tomorrow onwards no one will be there to help you. Enjoy your day and night in this room. Next time you will be afraid to talk in front of me. You will beg for forgiveness. Get that in your mind." He held my wrist and walked to the small path which held the staircase. He stepped down slowly as it was full of dark and dust. I followed him silently as I knew he would not listen to me. If I apologise a number of times also he will not spare me today. I got that so I stopped requesting him.

He switched on the light after searching for it for a few minutes. He did not leave my hand as he feared I may run. I want to run from here but I can't change my fate.

"Now you will live here for a few days till I will be convinced that you will follow all my rules. I am not like you who is the reason of our loved ones death." He said to me gritting his teeth with each word standing so close to me an inch gap between our faces. I was shocked by his words. How can he say I am the cause of my mothers death? My face dried with tears. One last look at him with my pained expression asking what did I do? But he did not give me any answer to my question. One stray tear left my eye while he was glaring at me. He turned sideways and left my hand. Without turning back he ran fast climbing the stairs and locking the room. I ran after him but he shut down the door on my face.

I climbed down the stairs and looked everywhere in the room to escape. It was a small room with cemented walls. Only dark surrounded and dust filled the room as it is not cleaned from so many days looking at it. There is another door and on one side of the wall. I moved forward and opened the door to find out that it was a bathroom. The smell is awful. I immediately closed that door as the smell made me nauseous. Only four walls surrounded me and a small yellow light bulb arranged in the middle of the room. I don't know when the light will go off as it is looking like it will go off any minute seeing its condition. There is no fan here. I don't know how I will manage here. But I have to bear it with patience.

I looked for a place to sit and searched for the cloth if it may be available to dust the floor clean. But I got none so I dusted with my hands at the corner of the room and rubbed my hands on my saree to clean my hands. I sat in the corner in indian style while drinking in my own thoughts interwining my palms together. I tapped my thighs to not think about anything. But my mind wanders off to Ayush of why he is doing this to me. Why is he behaving bipolar? If he has any problem he can ask me directly. I will answer him. What revenge he is speaking of I dont understand. I will ask him when he comes to me.

I came out of my thoughts when I heard a small sound. I was shivering. I know what this sounds like. I stood straight and saw who was making the sound.

"Ah..Ahh Mamma." I screamed so loudly as I saw a big rat looking at me. I ran towards the stairs fast and climbed up and banged the door to open it.

"Open the door. There is a big rat. Ayush Open the door damnit. Open. Open. Open." I am crying vigorously but no one is there to help me. I sat down adjacent to the door. I am shivering badly. I am really afraid of animals. I like seeing them from afar as I am really afraid of any kind of animal whether it is small or big.

I will not go down as the sound can be heard continuously in the room. My fear got the best of me as my silent sobs and whimpering came to an end after a few hours.

"Papa where are you? I really miss you. I miss you. Why did you leave me? I don't want to live with him, papa. He is very cruel papa. Please take me away from here papa. I will not leave you papa. Please take me away from this life papa. He is a monster papa. You don't know how he beat me. I will never go to him, papa. Please take me away." My dried tears came to an end and I am thinking about my papa who is my hero in my life. How he used to take care of my small little things. I whispered to myself thinking if my papa listens to my pleas. I slept on it curling myself thinking it would be a nightmare.

CPSIA information can be obtained
at www.ICGtesting.com
Printed in the USA
LVHW082255310123
738108LV00014BD/853

9 781837 619863